'I'll fight for m

Jack exhaled slowly.
stay on your right si

She gave him a rueful smile. 'Sorry. When hospital politics interfere with my patients it drives me round the bend. I shouldn't be taking it out on you.'

'Sounds to me as if you need chocolate,' he said, producing a bar from the pocket of his white coat. 'Catch.'

'Thanks.' She broke off a square, smiled, and threw the rest of the bar back to him. 'Perhaps it's my lucky day after all—having a Special Reg who can read my mind.'

They exchanged a glance and her smile faded. On second thoughts, she hoped he couldn't read her mind. Because chocolate wasn't what she wanted right then. She wanted Jack Sawyer's arms round her. And that beautiful mouth teasing hers...

Kate Hardy lives on the outskirts of Norwich with her husband, two small children, two lazy spaniels—and too many books to count! She wrote her first book at age six, when her parents gave her a typewriter for her birthday. She had the first of a series of sexy romances published at twenty-five and swapped a job in marketing communications for freelance health journalism when her son was born, so she could spend more time with him. She's wanted to write for Mills & Boon since she was twelve—and when she was pregnant with her daughter her husband pointed out that writing Medical Romances™ would be the perfect way to combine her interest in health issues with her love of good stories. It really is the best of both worlds—especially as she gets to meet a new gorgeous hero every time... Kate is always delighted to hear from readers—do drop in to her website at www.katehardy.com

Recent titles by the same author:

THE DOCTOR'S RESCUE
THE ITALIAN DOCTOR'S PROPOSAL
HER SPECIAL CHILD
HIS EMERGENCY FIANCÉE
A BABY OF HER OWN

THE HEART CONSULTANT'S LOVER

BY
KATE HARDY

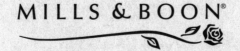

MILLS & BOON®

For Fi—best friend and godmother extraordinaire—
with much love

*First published in Great Britain 2004
Harlequin Mills & Boon Limited,
Eton House, 18-24 Paradise Road, Richmond, Surrey TW9 1SR*

© Pamela Brooks 2004

ISBN 0 263 83894 3

*Set in Times Roman 10½ on 12 pt.
03-0404-46271*

*Printed and bound in Spain
by Litografia Rosés, S.A., Barcelona*

PROLOGUE

No way was she going to get the car into that tiny space next to the massive concrete pillar. And Seb would kill her if there was a single speck of dirt on his precious car, let alone a scratch. As for a dent... He'd still murder her. Just slowly.

Maybe she should have stayed away. This was Fate's way of telling her that it was the wrong thing to do. If she'd been meant to get the job, her car wouldn't have had a flat battery, she'd have been at Calderford General in plenty of time to park, and she wouldn't have got a speeding ticket just outside Edinburgh either.

'Serves you right, Miranda Turner, for thinking you could come home on your own terms,' she muttered.

The knock on her window almost gave her heart failure. And it took her ages to wind down the steamed-up window.

'Are you OK, or are you lost?' a voice enquired.

Oh, no. She knew that look. *What's she doing in a car like that if she can't drive it?* Every time she'd driven Seb's car, she'd had the same reaction—men either scoffed or made sure they overtook her.

On the other hand...maybe this might be the lucky break she needed. She smiled sweetly and put on her best fluffy-and-feminine voice. 'I know it's terribly feeble of me, but it's not actually my car. And I've always been so hopeless at parking.' She fiddled with her hair. 'And that space is so *tiny!*'

5

He looked at her in seeming disbelief, then at the space. 'It is a bit tight,' he allowed.

She batted her eyelashes at him. 'I know it's a terrible imposition, but would you be kind enough to…?' Hopefully the chance to get behind the wheel of a vintage MG Roadster would be enough to make him say yes.

It was. 'Sure.'

Gratefully, she grabbed her handbag and hopped out of the car. And watched him park the damned thing in one fluid movement. Easy-peasy, lemon-squeezy. Why couldn't *she* do it? But she never had been able to park cars. Not since the day she'd passed her driving test, borrowed her mother's car and scraped it in the car park. Her father had gone bananas. Ever since then Miranda would rather have abseiled blindfolded down the Angel of the North, the huge sculpture just outside Newcastle, than park a car.

'Thank you,' she said as he handed her the car keys. 'I really do appreciate it.'

'No problem. Are you here to visit someone?'

You could say that, Miranda thought. She smiled at him. 'Mmm.'

'The hospital entrance is over there—if you ask at Reception, they'll direct you to the ward you need,' he told her kindly, pointing to the large domed building across the other side of the car park. 'And you'll need a ticket—they're pretty hot on fines.'

Now she felt horrible. He wasn't a chauvinist pig at all. He was a nice bloke who'd helped her out of a mess. A nice bloke with a gorgeous smile and…

Stop right there, she told herself crossly. She'd probably never see him again. The way her day was going, she wouldn't be in the North East again for a very long time, let alone Calderford. And she wasn't in the market for a man in any case. Since Rupert, she didn't do serious relationships. 'Thanks for the warning,' she said lightly.

She didn't really have time to get a ticket. But then again, she wasn't going to get the job so it didn't really matter if she was late for her interview. She was lucky she'd even got this far. Because no way would Ralph Turner, clinical director and head of paediatrics, let his only child get a consultant's post in the cardiology department. Not in *his* hospital.

With a rueful smile, she headed for the ticket machine.

CHAPTER ONE

'I REALLY don't know why we all have to sit here, waiting for her,' Jack said, his mouth compressed into a tight line. 'I've got a ward round to do. And I want to check on Imogen Parker.'

'It's Miss Turner's first day and she's called a meeting of all the coronary care unit staff,' Leila Ward, the senior sister, reminded him. 'Obviously she wants to introduce herself and meet the team.'

'Yeah. *If* she turns up on time.'

Leila patted his hand. 'Don't be such a grouch. I know you're disappointed you didn't get the job, but give her a chance.'

'Right.' Jack rolled his eyes. 'But remember who we're talking about. Her dad's the clinical director of Calderford General.'

'She might be nice. She might be extremely competent. She might be better than you,' Leila pointed out. 'Which might be why she got the consultant's job.'

'"Might" being the operative word.' Jack sighed at the look on his colleague's face. 'OK, OK, I'll give her a chance. But if she's late or incompetent, or it turns out to be a case of a job for the boss's daughter, don't expect me to keep my mouth shut.'

'It might help if you start with it closed,' Leila whispered as the new consultant walked in and Jack's jaw dropped.

It was *her*. The girl with the sports car. The girl who couldn't park.

Ms Fluffy.

Except…she didn't look in the slightest bit fluffy this time. She was wearing a business suit, albeit with a short skirt; that glorious dark hair was pulled back severely at the nape of her neck; and she was wearing oval glasses with narrow metal frames. If she was wearing any make-up at all, it was so understated that it was barely there. She looked serious and studious—and *competent*.

Or maybe she was Ms Fluffy's sister. No way could someone change their image just like that! When she glanced quickly round the room, she didn't give the slightest indication that she recognised anyone—and surely she would have remembered him as the person who'd got her out of a fix in the car park the other week?

His mouth compressed further. Or maybe she was just so used to people doing what she wanted that she hadn't given him a second's further thought. Not that it should bother him. He wasn't interested in Miranda Turner anyway.

Of all the people, in all the hospital, Miranda thought, her knight in shining armour *would* have to work on her ward! Which meant that she was going to have to play this very, very carefully.

No. She was just going to be honest. She'd leave the games to her father.

She took a deep breath, psyching herself up for the speech she knew she had to make. 'Good morning, everyone. Thanks for making it—and I promise not to keep you long. I just wanted to introduce myself properly. I'm Miranda Turner, and I'm delighted to be joining you here at Calderford General.' She smiled. This was the nasty bit. 'You've probably guessed by now that Ralph Turner is my father. Believe me, being interviewed by someone who knows all the most embarrassing things about you is a nightmare! Luckily, he couldn't vote on my appointment because of the family connection.' Hopefully that would squash any rumours that she'd only got the job because of who she was, not what she could do.

She smiled again. 'I've already met one of you, though I didn't know it at the time.' She gestured to her champion. 'He rescued me in the car park when I realised I'd left my shoehorn at home and couldn't get the car into the smallest space in the world.'

To her relief, one or two of them actually laughed.

'I can assure you, I'm a much better doctor than I am a driver. I'm really looking forward to working with you—and I'd like to invite everyone on the ward for a drink on Friday night in the Calderford Arms at seven, so I can start getting to know you better. In the meantime, I've restocked the biscuit and coffee supplies in the kitchen.' She glanced round again. No overt hostility—except from her rescuer. His face was expressionless but his eyes definitely weren't friendly.

'Some of you might be worried that I'm going to do the new-broom thing, and make changes just so it looks as if I'm actually doing something. That's not the way I work,' she said. 'I've spent the last seven years in Cardiology at Glasgow, so I might be able to bring some new ideas in—but you might be able to teach me new things, too. I believe in teamwork, and I hope you'll see me as just another team member.'

She couldn't help looking at her rescuer again. And 'no chance' was written all over his face. She sighed inwardly. Time. She just had to give it time. 'Thanks, everyone. I'll catch up with you all individually during the day.'

*   *   *

She was good. He had to give her that. She'd told the car park story against herself before anyone else could—attack being the best form of defence. And she was clearly going out of her way to be friendly, asking the whole ward to a welcome drink at the pub near the hospital. But he still couldn't quite forgive her for lying to him, saying that she was visiting someone. Why couldn't she just have said that she was going for an interview?

An interview for the same job he'd gone for. The job he hadn't got. And how long would it be before he had another chance to show his family that all those sacrifices had been worth it? Maybe a few months, until she got bored and moved on. Or maybe longer if she decided she liked it, or her father wanted her to stay… He sighed inwardly. He knew he had to be flexible if he wanted his career to take the fast track—he had to be prepared to move to where the opportunities were—but how could he possibly leave Calderford?

'Hello.'

She sounded a little unsure of herself. Jack hardened his heart and gave her a professional nod. 'Ms Turner.'

'It's Miranda,' she said, holding out her hand. 'And I wanted to apologise. About the car thing.' She made a face. 'Interview nerves.'

'Yeah.' Unwillingly, he took her hand to shake it. Then wished he hadn't when a spark of awareness jolted his whole body.

Oh, no. Oh, no, no, no. Nothing could possibly happen between them. He wasn't even going to start thinking about his boss in those sorts of terms. And even if she hadn't been his boss, nothing could happen between them. They lived in completely different worlds, and he really wasn't into the lifestyle of the rich and pampered. He'd been there, done that and learned the hard way that it wasn't for him. No way was he ever going to get involved with a posh girl again. Jessica's words had burned into his soul, the giggled conversation he'd overheard with her friends. *Jack? Yeah, he's drop-dead gorgeous. But Mummy's right. He's from the wrong side of town— fun for now, but he's not the kind of man you'd marry.*

Then he realised he was still holding Miranda's hand. He dropped it as if he'd been scalded. Hell. He didn't want her to think he'd lost his concentration because of— well, because he *fancied* her. She might be beautiful but she wasn't his type. Besides, he wasn't looking for a relationship. Not until he'd reached consultant level. He wouldn't be the kind of man a woman wanted to marry until then. 'Sorry, I didn't catch what you said.'

'Just that I really did appreciate you rescuing me.'

She sounded sincere. And her body language matched her words. Now he felt horrible. Perhaps Miranda Turner wasn't the hard, manipulative woman he'd assumed she was. Or maybe his judgement was just out of kilter. She might seem nice now—but, then again, so had Jessica.

'And I'd like to join you on the ward round, if that's OK with you, Dr Sawyer.'

She'd clearly read his name from his badge, and he could tell she was waiting for him to say, 'Call me Jack.' Well, she'd have to wait a bit longer, until he could see what she was really made of. Whether she'd really got the job on merit.

'And I'm perfectly happy for you to lead—you know the patients and the staff better than I do.'

She didn't say it but he knew what she meant. *At the moment.* 'Right.'

'Shall we?'

*   *   *

'In Room One, we have Imogen Parker. She has unstable angina,' Jack said.

Unstable angina. No. Oh, no. Of all the things she had to face, why did *that* have to be her first case on her new ward? Miranda shook herself, knowing that she had to put the memories behind her. Now wasn't the time or place to think about what had happened to May. Her patient had to come first.

With angina pectoris, the heart muscle didn't get enough blood and oxygen to meet its needs, so the patient felt tightness or a burning sensation in the chest when climbing stairs or walking. In more severe cases, known as unstable angina, the patient felt pain on resting, too. 'She had an ECG when she came in, and a cardiac stress test a while back,' Jack told Miranda. An ECG or electrocardiogram measured the electrical activity in the heart; the stress test was a second ECG while the patient walked fast enough on a treadmill to cause chest pain. Both could show up current heart problems or previous heart attacks. 'They were both normal.'

'What about blood tests?' Miranda asked. They might show an underlying cause for the angina.

Jack nodded. 'They're clear. No signs of polycythaemia, thyrotoxicosis or hyperlipidaemia.' So Imogen Parker's blood didn't have an abnormally large amount of red blood cells, she didn't have an inflamed thyroid gland and there weren't abnormally high levels of fat in her blood. 'Not diabetes or anaemia either,' he added.

'What about her angiography?' Miranda asked. It was standard procedure in these cases to take an X-ray of the blood vessels around the patient's heart.

'It showed a slight narrowing of a couple of the blood vessels.'

'Is she on GTN?' GTN, or glyceryl trinitrate, increased

the flow of blood through the heart muscle and controlled the symptoms of angina.

'It gave her headaches, so she's on beta-blockers,' Jack said. 'Her GP's worried as the drugs weren't working that well and she's still getting pain on rest, so we're keeping an eye on her.'

'So you're thinking about surgical intervention?'

'Possibly.'

They went into the room. 'Good morning, Miss Parker,' Jack said with a smile. 'I'd like to introduce our new consultant, Miss Turner.'

'Miranda,' she corrected. 'May I?' She indicated the edge of the bed.

'Of course, Doctor,' the old lady said.

'May I call you Imogen?'

Imogen nodded.

Miranda sat down and held the elderly woman's hand. Imogen Parker was even around the same age that May would have been—in her late seventies. This was way too close for comfort. 'Jack tells me we're keeping an eye on the pain you've been having lately. How are you feeling today, Imogen?'

'Not so bad,' Imogen said quietly.

The slight greyness in her face told Jack and Miranda otherwise. Jack flicked quickly through her chart. 'You had another two attacks last night?'

'It was nothing, really.' Imogen made a dismissive gesture. 'I don't like to bother the nurses. They're busy.'

'They'd be a lot more bothered if they thought you weren't feeling well and hadn't told them,' Miranda said. That was precisely what May had done. And then it had been too late. 'Imogen, trust me—you're not making a nuisance of yourself if you call them. They're here to help you.'

'So when can I go home?' Imogen asked.

'I can't tell you right now,' Miranda said. 'Dr Sawyer and I need to talk about how your drugs are working and what we can do to stop the pain coming back so frequently. Do you have anyone to look after you at home?'

'My Floss—she's my little Westie. She hates being in kennels.'

Jack and Miranda exchanged a glance. 'If you tell me where she's staying, I'll ring the kennels for you and find out how she's doing,' Miranda said.

'She's at Berrybank, on the other side of Calderford.'

'I'll ring them at lunchtime for an update, and I'll get a phone brought in so you can hear it for yourself.'

'Would you?' Imogen's eyes glittered with tears. 'Thank you, love.'

'No problem.' Miranda squeezed her hand. 'We'll be back to see you a bit later on. And if you feel even the slightest twinge, promise me you'll press your buzzer.'

'I will.'

'Thank you. Is there anything you'd like to add, Jack?'

He shook his head. 'We'll see you later, Miss Parker.'

'Does she have any relatives nearby?' Miranda asked as they left the room.

'There's a great-niece who's either phoned or popped in every day.'

Oh, yes. Miranda knew all about great-nieces being the only ones in the family who cared enough to check on their elderly great-aunt.

'But apparently she has three under-fives.'

'So Imogen can't stay with her—the niece already has enough on her plate, and you can't expect small children to give an elderly woman the peace and quiet she needs while she recovers.'

'You're really going to ring the kennels?' Jack asked.

'If she's worrying, it's likely to bring on another angina attack,' Miranda said. Jack didn't need to know the other reason: that she wanted to do for Imogen what she'd failed to do for May. 'I'll go and see the dog myself, if it'll help her—maybe bring her a photograph so she doesn't feel quite so alone.'

This definitely wasn't the attitude he'd been expecting. Jack had a nasty feeling that he'd underestimated Miranda Turner. 'Maybe,' he said, wishing he'd thought of it in the first place. One little phone call would make a big difference to their patient's mental state—and that would make an even bigger difference to her ability to deal with the physical problem. He really should have thought of that himself.

'Next, we have Sidney Patterson. He has a thoracic aortic aneurysm,' Jack continued as they stood outside Room Two. 'He hadn't had any specific symptoms but he'd gone for a routine check-up and the GP suspected something was up and sent him for a CT scan.' An aortic aneurysm—a bulge in the wall of the main artery carrying blood from the heart—didn't always cause symptoms, depending on which part of the artery it affected. Sometimes the patient had difficulty swallowing or was hoarse because it pressed on a nerve controlling a vocal cord; if it was further down in the abdomen, it sometimes caused backache. 'It's around seven centimetres in diameter, so he's booked in for surgery on Friday afternoon.'

Miranda nodded. Aneurysms of that size were more prone to rupture, and there was a high mortality rate. She glanced at his notes. 'He's a prime candidate, isn't he? Mid-fifties, male, high blood pressure, atherosclerosis.' She paused. 'We ran some trials in my last hospital to repair aneurysms without major open surgery. One was on keyhole surgery, and the other was putting a catheter into the artery at the groin which carried an endovascular stent to the aneurysm.'

'Then you leave the stent in place to support the aneurysm,' Jack said thoughtfully. 'I'd like to see some studies on that. But here we take the open-surgery approach, using Dacron tubing.' The tubing supported the aneurysm and stopped it growing any bigger.

'Fair enough,' Miranda said. 'Keyhole surgery and endovascular stents are still fairly experimental and need controlled trials. But maybe we can consider them as options in the future.'

So much for her speech about new brooms. She really was trying to prove herself the hotshot, wasn't she? 'If the clinical director agrees to a research proposal,' he reminded her.

She gave a rueful smile. 'He's going to need a lot of persuasion.'

Jack couldn't help himself. 'Then you're the right person to do it, aren't you?' And then he wished he hadn't said it when he saw her flinch. Just momentarily. Nothing in her manner changed—but he knew he'd hurt her. He might just as well have said to her straight that she'd only got her job because of who she was.

She made no comment, simply went into Room Two. And Sid was as charmed by Miranda as Mrs Parker had been. 'So are you going to be the one with me under the knife, Dr Turner?'

Jack noticed that she didn't correct him that she was 'Miss'. 'Fraid not,' she said with a smile. 'You're in Dr Sawyer's very capable hands—actually, I'm assisting him.'

She was going to assist *him*? Since when? Or was she

trying to prove that she wasn't going to take over completely?

'So tell me, Mr Patterson, how are you getting on with keeping your blood pressure down?'

He shrugged. 'I'm taking the tablets, love.'

She grinned. 'How many times do you forget them?'

'Ooh, let me see—I forget,' he teased back.

'And you're cutting your cholesterol levels?'

'The wife's in charge of that. Though I miss my bacon sandwiches at lunchtime.'

'The odd one won't hurt you. Dieting's tough,' Miranda said, 'and if you feel deprived, you're more likely to crack and have a binge.'

'Especially when you smell bacon cooking.'

She chuckled. 'Tell me about it. But make sure it's grilled, it's lean and any visible fat's removed, and the bread's wholemeal.' She glanced at his fingers. 'And I don't have to nag you about the cigarettes, do I?'

'My daughter threw away all my duty-frees,' he said ruefully. 'No one else in the house smokes, so they can smell if I've slipped up. And I know I won't hear the end of it if I do.'

'Sounds as if you're in good hands,' she said with a grin.

Then they saw the rest of the patients on the unit, starting with a woman who'd contracted bacterial endocarditis following a routine tooth extraction—she was near the end of a six-week course of antibiotics and the unit was checking to see whether her heart valve would need surgery. The other patients had recently had heart attacks—one was still very recent so he was under observation in Room Four and the man in Room Five was ready to move down to the general ward.

'Right. Coffee and a quick confab?' Miranda asked when Jack had signed the discharge notes.

'Sure.'

'How do you take your coffee?' she asked as they headed for the kitchen.

'Black, no sugar.'

'Same as me. Good. That'll make life easy.' She poured them both a coffee, topped up the water in the filter machine and handed him a mug. 'My office?'

'Sure.' Was she pushy or just efficient? Jack wanted to think it was the former, but he had a niggling feeling that it was the latter. And then he had an even more niggling feeling: he admired her for it. Oh, hell. Why couldn't Miranda Turner be just an ordinary person? Why did she have to be the clinical director's daughter? Why had she had to come onto his ward and throw his brain into chaos?

'Right, then. Sid's having surgery on Friday; Jane's awaiting tests with a query valve replacement; Joe's under obs and Martyn's going home.' She ticked the cases off on her fingers.

Definitely efficient, Jack thought. She didn't waste words.

'That leaves Imogen. Her angina's unstable and the drugs aren't working.' She flipped through the file and looked at the angiography results. 'We've got two options—a bypass graft or an angioplasty.' An angioplasty was where a small balloon was inserted in the narrowed artery and inflated so it flattened out the fatty plaques lining the blood vessel.

'Angioplasties often have to be repeated and a bypass gives better symptom control,' Jack said.

'But if she has a bypass it'll take her longer to recover and she'll have to stay here longer—which will worry her more, because of her dog. And worry leads to higher blood pressure—'

'Which increases her risk of a heart attack,' Jack finished.

'Given her age, and the fact that only a couple of the vessels show narrowing—here and here—I'd prefer an angioplasty. It's not quite so invasive so it'll be less of a shock to her system, and the newer heparinised stents lower the risk of a heart attack.'

'And if it doesn't work?'

'Then we'll have to do a bypass.' She looked levelly at him. 'Do you think a bypass is the better option?'

He shook his head. 'We'll play it your way.'

'No. We're a team. We do what we agree is best for the patient. Ego doesn't come into it,' she said crisply.

Jack sucked his teeth. 'And that's telling me.'

Her eyes narrowed. 'I don't like playing games, Dr Sawyer. If you have a problem with me, let's get it out in the open now.'

'Is it that obvious?'

'That you resent me? Yes. Though I don't know what I've done to upset you—apart from the car-park incident, and I've already apologised for that. Besides, it was a win-win situation.'

He lifted his chin. 'How do you work that out?'

'We both got what we wanted. You were all too happy to park the Roadster, and I got the car parked without a scratch on it so Seb didn't murder me.'

Her boyfriend? Even though it was none of his business—and he shouldn't even *want* to know anyway—he couldn't help asking. 'Seb?'

'My next-door neighbour in Glasgow.'

No reason for his heart to give that little lurch of relief. No reason at all.

'My car decided not to start the day of the interview. Seb took pity on me and lent me the Roadster—on condition there wasn't so much as a speck of dust on it when I got back.'

Was that a glint of mischief in her eyes? He couldn't tell. 'You believe in straight talking, don't you?'

'It makes life simpler.'

He nodded. 'OK. Then you may as well know that I went for this job, too.'

'And you think I got it because I'm Ralph Turner's daughter.'

'I didn't say that.'

'But it's what you're thinking.' She shrugged. 'I got the job because of what I can do, not for who I am.'

'On the round, you sounded as if you knew what you were talking about.'

'Well, thanks for the vote of confidence,' she said dryly.

'And that came out badly. I didn't mean it like that.' He sighed. 'We've got off to a bad start.'

'Look, I'm sorry you didn't get the job, but I hope it's not going to cause us problems working together. From my point of view, I get a special reg who knows exactly what he's doing. From your point of view, I'm not going to change the way you work—and you can get on with being a doctor and leave the hospital politics to someone else. So, let's start again. Perhaps, this time, we can do it on first-name terms.' She held out her hand. 'I'm Miranda Turner. Pleased to meet you, Jack.'

'Pleased to meet you, Miranda.' Jack took her proffered hand. 'I've seen your résumé. If that didn't convince me, the ward round proved you know your stuff.'

She didn't push for a grovelling apology, he noticed. She just gave him a quick smile. 'Thanks.'

Jack refused to acknowledge the beat his heart had just missed. Nothing was going to happen between them. They were colleagues and that was it. And even if Miranda hadn't been the professor's daughter, he'd already learned his lesson with Jessica. The hard way. 'I'll ring Jordan Francis—he's our theatre manager, if you haven't met him yet—and see if he can fit us in tomorrow.'

'If Imogen agrees,' Miranda added. 'We need to talk to her great-niece as well. I don't want to send her home without any support.' Not after what had happened to May. 'Perhaps there's someone else in the family who can help. Or maybe Imogen could stay in a convalescent home short term, then we can arrange to get someone to look in on her at set times when she comes home and take her dog for a walk.' She glanced at her watch. 'Speaking of which, I need to phone the kennels.'

By the time they'd finished writing up their notes, Jack had booked theatre time and Miranda had reassured Imogen that Floss was fine, it was nearly lunchtime.

'So, are you having lunch with your father?' Jack asked.

'You must be joking!' Was that a look of horror on her face or was it his imagination? When he looked again, her expression had been carefully schooled into neutral. 'I doubt if he'd have time.'

'On your first day?'

She shrugged. 'Would you expect him to have lunch with any other consultant on their first day?'

'Well—maybe not. But you're his daughter.' If he'd been in her position, his mother would have had lunch booked from the word go. His father… Well, Jack tried not to think about his father. But any normal father would make sure she'd settled in OK, surely?

'Here I'm a doctor. Family doesn't come into it.'

Was she upset about that? Or was she the one who'd insisted on it? Jack couldn't quite work her out. 'So what are you doing?'

'I thought I'd go for a walk, get some fresh air. Maybe grab a sandwich.'

He shrugged. 'I'm off to the canteen in twenty minutes, if you want to join me.'

'Are you being nice, or do you mean that?'

He couldn't help smiling. 'You're right. You *do* believe in straight talking.'

'And?'

It took him a bit by surprise, but… 'I meant it.'

'Good. You can tell me what not to pick in the canteen. And, as it's my first day, it'll be my shout.'

'You're on.'

Miranda sneaked a glance at Jack as she drank her coffee. Now they'd cleared the air, there was a good chance they'd have a decent working relationship.

And that's *working*, Miranda Turner, she emphasised to herself. Yes, Jack Sawyer was attractive, with intense dark eyes, dark hair, pale olive skin and the kind of smile that made her heart beat a little bit faster. Yes, he had a beautiful mouth, generous and soft. Yes, he had nice hands—clean, well-shaped fingernails, the kind of hands she could only too easily imagine stroking her skin and playing with her hair.

But imagination was as far as it could go. He was her colleague—her junior, to boot—and that made him off limits. Particularly as she was working in her father's hospital. Ralph Turner would be less than pleased to hear she was seeing one of her staff. It simply wasn't done. Besides, she'd already learned the hard way that rela-

tionships weren't for her. She was focused on her career.
Completely.

Jack kept both hands wrapped round his mug of coffee.
This was crazy. He wasn't in the market for a relationship. Even if he had been, his boss was the *last* person
he should be thinking about.

And yet… Oh, hell. Behave, he told his libido. So what
if her eyes are the colour of the sea on a winter's day?
So what if her mouth is a perfect Cupid's bow? And
don't even think about reaching over to unpin her hair
and letting it fall over her shoulders like rippling oiled
silk. Just concentrate on the fact that she's your boss. She
may be efficient, straight-talking and think on her feet—
everything you like in a woman—but laying so much as
a finger on her would be professional suicide. You've
worked hard to get as far as you have—don't blow it
now just because you fancy her. Stay away, he warned
himself. Hands off.

CHAPTER TWO

BY THE start of her shift on Wednesday, Miranda felt as if she'd always worked at Calderford General. All the staff on the coronary care unit seemed to accept her as part of the team—including Jack, she thought with relief—and she'd settled into the ward routine.

Wednesday morning's angina clinic flew by and Miranda kept her lunch-break short, to make sure she was on time for her theatre appointment with Imogen Parker. But just before Imogen was due to have her pre-med, the phone rang in Miranda's office.

'Miranda Turner.'

'Hi, Miranda, it's Jordan Francis.'

There was only one reason she could think of why the theatre manager would call her. 'Hi, Jordan. I hope you're not going to tell me there's a problem with my two o'clock,' she said, keeping her voice light.

''Fraid so.'

'Majax?' she asked, using the hospital's shorthand term for 'major accident' or 'major incident'—meaning that the A and E department needed all the theatre slots to deal with surgical emergencies.

'Um, no.'

She picked up on the slight trace of guilt in his voice. 'Jordan, I know it's not your fault, but CCU booked that slot for a reason. If there isn't a major emergency, why are you pulling the slot?'

'The prof needs it.'

'Why?' she asked, knowing that she was putting the theatre manager on the spot but unable to stop herself.

Jordan sounded uncomfortable. 'He's booked a demonstration.'

'Oh, has he?' she said crossly. 'Don't tell me—he said I wouldn't mind.' She scowled. She should have guessed her father would pull a stunt like this. Well, he'd soon find that she wasn't a pushover any more. 'Jordan, I'm sorry. I shouldn't take it out on you. Thanks for letting me know. When's the next available two-hour slot?'

'Friday morning, half-past nine. Do you want me to book you in?'

'Yes, please. And, Jordan?'

'Yes?'

'If anyone tries to override it—unless it's a majax—can you refer them to me, please?'

'Sure.'

'Cheers.'

'Um, Miranda, I was wondering…would you like to come out for a drink with me? Or dinner, or something?'

'Yes, that'd be nice.'

'Tomorrow?'

'Sorry. I'm on a late. How about Monday?'

'Great. I'll book somewhere…say, for seven? And do you like Italian?'

'Seven's fine and I love Italian—thanks. Talk to you soon.'

She cut the connection, rang the professor's secretary and asked to speak to him.

'I'm afraid he's with someone, Miranda. He's on his way to a demonstration.'

'It'll only take ten seconds, Ally. Promise. And it's urgent. I wouldn't ask otherwise.'

'All right. As it's you.'

A second later, a testy voice informed her, 'Miranda, I don't have time to talk to you right now. I'm about to do a demonstration.'

'I know. In *my* theatre slot.'

'For heaven's sake, you were only doing an angioplasty. It's a routine operation. You can reschedule.'

'My patient has unstable angina.' Didn't that mean anything to him? Had he forgotten May so easily? 'If she has an MI before I can do the angioplasty, I'll have to do an emergency bypass and I don't want to put her through that.'

'It's not that likely, and you're making a fuss.'

'Too right I am, Professor.'

His voice hardened. 'Don't you take that tone with me. I'm your father.'

'We're at work. Which means I'm a doctor first and your daughter second.'

'Miranda, I don't have time for this!'

She knew exactly what *that* meant. 'Don't tell me— you discussed it over lunch, thought it was a good idea, saw my name on the list and decided that I'd make the least fuss about losing my slot. Wrong. I expect exactly the same treatment—the same *courtesy*—as you'd give any of your other consultants. Why didn't you ask me first?'

'We'll talk about this later.'

'Fine. And you'll have my formal letter of complaint on your desk when you get back.'

'This demonstration's important. It could bring money into the hospital.'

'And money's more important than a patient's health?' Miranda asked scornfully. 'This wasn't an elective op. I'd have understood if there was a majax, but a *demo*?

Why couldn't your VIPs watch one of the scheduled operations?'

'Don't be difficult.'

She could feel her blood pressure rising. After all the years she'd spent training—all the exams she'd taken—he still treated her like a four-year-old who knew nothing, instead of a highly qualified thirty-two-year-old. 'Difficult? Some would say I was a chip off the old block. Though from the days when he cared about people more than politics,' she informed him sharply. 'Enjoy your demo.' She put the phone down before she really lost her temper.

She was still shaking when she saw Leila and asked her to hold the pre-med.

'Are you OK?' the senior sister asked.

'Fine,' Miranda lied. 'I'll explain to Imogen that her operation's been rescheduled then I'll be in my office, if anyone needs me. I may as well get stuck into the paperwork now I'm not in Theatre.'

She'd just printed off her carefully composed letter to her father when there was a rap on her door. She looked up to see Jack standing in the doorway 'You OK?' he asked.

'Fine,' she said tightly.

His raised eyebrow said it all. She sighed. 'Sorry. I'm just annoyed that our slot was pulled at the last minute. I've rescheduled Imogen's op for Friday morning.'

'Don't tell me—A and E?' he asked.

'Nope. Politics.' She signed the letter with a flourish. 'And this is a complaint letter. I'm just going to take it down to Ally.'

'Pulling strings with the Prof?'

How could he even *think* that she'd go running off to Daddy at the first sign of trouble? 'The Prof,' she said in disgust, 'is the one who took our slot—without having the courtesy to ask us. The complaint's *about* him.'

'Ah.'

'Don't worry, you won't be caught in the crossfire.' She folded her arms. 'The Prof just needs reminding that I'm not a yes person. And I'll fight for my ward's rights.'

Jack exhaled slowly. 'I think I'll make sure I stay on your right side. Shall I ask Leila to pass the word round that you turn into Attila the Hun when someone crosses you?'

The tension suddenly drained from her, and she gave him a rueful smile. 'Sorry. When hospital politics interfere with my patients, it drives me round the bend. I shouldn't be taking it out on you.'

'Sounds to me as if you need chocolate,' he said, producing a bar from the pocket of his white coat. 'Catch.'

'Thanks.' She broke off a square, smiled and threw the rest of the bar back to him. 'Perhaps it's my lucky day after all—having a special reg who can read my mind.'

They exchanged a glance and her smile faded. On second thoughts, she hoped he couldn't read her mind. Because chocolate wasn't what she wanted right then. She wanted Jack Sawyer's arms round her. And that beautiful mouth teasing hers…

No. She had to keep a very tight rein on her imagination, or it would play havoc with her work. 'Thanks for the chocolate. I needed that. I'll just drop this off— I'll be five minutes, max. Bleep me if you need me.'

'OK, boss.'

The 'boss' had been more for his benefit than hers, Jack thought. Because when he'd seen her sitting there, angry and upset on their patient's behalf, he'd wanted to put his arms round her, tell her that everything would be all right. Hold her close. And to hell with his job.

* * *

'I will not tolerate this!' Ralph stormed, waving the piece of paper at his daughter. 'What do you think you were doing?'

'Exactly what I told you I'd do. Complaining about your behaviour. In future, I expect professional courtesy from you *as a member of your staff*,' she emphasised.

His eyes narrowed. 'Don't play games with me.'

'I'm beyond that,' she said crisply. 'This is about my ward. My patients come first.'

'You sound like May.'

Miranda smiled. 'Thanks for the compliment.' Even though it had been given grudgingly—and she wasn't entirely sure he'd meant it as a compliment. She knew he hadn't ever really forgiven May for stepping in when Miranda had been eighteen.

'You're impossible. This is exactly why I didn't want you working here.'

'Because I'm not a yes person? I don't think Jack Sawyer is either. Though if he'd got the job, you wouldn't have taken his theatre slot without asking, would you?'

'As clinical director, I have to make unpopular decisions.'

'Agreed. But they don't have to be stupid ones.'

'Miranda,' Ralph said warningly.

'Professor, I know you won't admit it, but you were in the wrong. And if you do it again, I'll complain again—and I'll copy my letter to the CEO next time, as well as to Human Resources.'

'For your information—and not that I should have to explain myself to you—I'd booked the demo several weeks ago. Someone else needed the theatre I'd booked, because of the specialised equipment, and I had to move things around. Yours wasn't the only slot I moved.'

'Oh.' She flushed. She hadn't known that. Jordan hadn't told her.

'So I suggest you check your facts first next time before you write stroppy letters.'

She took a deep breath. But before she could apologise there was a rap on the door and Jack came in.

'Sorry—I'll come back later,' he said.

'Not at all. We've finished. Come in, my boy,' Ralph said.

Miranda's stomach lurched at the words. *My boy*. She wasn't his boy—and never could be. The tone, too, was different: when he called her 'my girl', it meant he was putting her in her place, not being genial and proud.

'I wanted to see you anyway,' Ralph continued, smiling at Jack.

Why didn't the professor ever smile at *her* like that?

'We've got a little one coming into Paeds tomorrow. Possible tetralogy of Fallot. I'd like you to take a look at her.'

Well, excuse me. *I'm* supposed to be the consultant here, Miranda thought. But her father had made it obvious that he respected Jack's abilities above her own.

'Is that OK with you?' Jack asked, looking at her. 'Or do you need me here?'

What could she say? If she said, no, he couldn't do it, they'd both think she was being petty—jealous even. The worst of it was, they'd be right. She *was* jealous of Jack, and the fact that the Professor clearly respected him. A respect he certainly didn't feel for his daughter. 'Fine,' she said tightly. 'Was there anything else you needed me for, Professor?'

'No.' His voice cooled noticeably as he looked at her. 'Just think about what I said.'

She nodded, her throat tight with misery. Same old,

same old. She'd thought by working with her father she'd finally persuade him to value her abilities. All she'd done had been to make things even worse between them.

When Ralph left, Miranda virtually snapped at Jack. 'So what can I do for you?'

He lifted his hands in surrender. 'Hey, what did I do?'

'Nothing.'

'Then what's the problem?' When she said nothing, he folded his arms. 'So much for straight talking.'

'If you must know, the Prof was tearing me off a strip. Apparently he'd booked the demonstration ages ago. Ours wasn't the only slot he'd moved.'

Jack shrugged. 'Might be better to check before you act next time.'

Her eyes narrowed. 'So you think I've been unreasonable?'

'Yes and no. You were right to challenge our slot being moved—but you should have made sure of your facts.' Maybe he should have warned her about Jordan's slapdash tendencies—though he'd tried to be fair and let her make up her own mind about their theatre manager instead of prejudicing her against him.

'Great. So you think I'm incompetent, too.'

Jack frowned. 'No, of course not.' And her father couldn't think it either, otherwise he wouldn't have let the others on the selection panel offer her the job. 'Just…you're playing a dangerous game.'

'So what am I supposed to do? Curry favour with the Prof?'

Was that what she thought he was doing, just because he'd agreed to go down to Paeds? It wasn't that at all. He was interested in paediatric cardiology—besides, he owed it to his family to get on as well as he could at the hospital. He wasn't going to turn down opportunities just because Miranda was having a private war with the Prof. Just in time, he stopped himself telling her that. It was none of her business. 'If you're going to argue with your father, that's up to you—but leave the ward out of it.'

Her eyes darkened. 'I'm not playing games.'

Yeah, right. And neither had Jessica, he thought bitterly. Except on a day with a Y in it. 'You asked my opinion. I gave it to you.'

'OK. I'm sorry. What did you want to see me about?'

He couldn't remember now. Not now she'd made him think of Jessica. 'Doesn't matter,' he said. 'Some other time.' He left, closing her office door and resisting the temptation to bang it. He was *not* going to let her get under his skin. In any way.

Thursday was less fraught, until Miranda promised to help their new student with setting up an ECG and reading the results.

'Dr Sawyer, can I borrow you for a second?' Miranda asked.

'Sure,' Jack said, with a smile that turned her knees temporarily to jelly. 'What's up?'

'I need a model. I'm walking Hannah through a 12-lead ECG, and she doesn't want to do it on a patient.'

'So you're just after my body?'

She wished he hadn't said that. The images his words brought to mind were way too disturbing—particularly after the way he'd smiled at her. But she wasn't going to let him know that he'd rattled her. 'That's right. Any old body'd do, but I thought Hannah might find a supposedly young and fit male easier for her first ECG,' she said, adopting the same light, teasing tone he'd used. 'Come into my office and strip to the waist.'

Definitely disturbing, she thought as Jack took off the

white coat, shirt and tie to reveal a perfectly toned torso and a light sprinkling of dark hair on his chest. Just pretend he's middle-aged with a paunch, she told herself. He may be gorgeous, but he's off limits. 'OK, Hannah. The V1 lead goes on the edge of the sternum, on the patient's right-hand side. Count down between the ribs until you get to the fourth intercostal space.'

'Here?' Hannah asked.

'Perfect. The V2 lead goes in the same place on the left-hand side.'

Hannah did as she was asked.

'Now we'll do the V4 lead. Why do you think I want to do that one next?'

'No idea,' Hannah admitted.

'V3 goes halfway between V2 and V4, so it's easier if you put V4 in place first,' Jack explained.

Miranda was forced to meet his eyes. She stopped herself blushing—just. She only hoped he wasn't a mind-reader—she definitely didn't want him knowing what she was thinking, right then. 'Exactly. V4 picks up the patient's apex beat. That's the point furthest from the manubrium—that's the hexagonal part at the .top of the breastbone—where we can still feel the heart beating. It's in the fifth intercostal space, in a line roughly halfway across the collar-bone.' She found the spot and her fingertips brushed lightly against Jack's skin. Just as well *he* was the one having the ECG, she thought. Her own heartbeat had just become extremely erratic, simply from touching him. This was crazy. He was her colleague. Her *junior*. She couldn't think like this about him. Particularly when she'd agreed to go on a date with someone else. This really, really wasn't good.

'Can you show me where you'd put V3?' she asked Hannah, avoiding looking at Jack.

Hannah nodded. 'Here.'

'Well done.' Miranda smiled at her. 'The rest of the leads go in a horizontal line with V4. V5 is here, in the anterior axillary line, and V7 is on the posterior axillary line. So V6 goes…?'

'Halfway between them?' Hannah guessed.

'Spot on,' Miranda said, then talked the junior doctor through placing the rest of the leads. 'Great. You're done.' She switched the monitor on. 'The trace shows the electrical activity of the heart so we can see what's going on. We can tell if someone has had a heart attack, and roughly when it was—in the last few hours, days, weeks or months.' She let the machine run until she had a strip of a dozen heartbeats, and turned it off. 'This is a good example of normal sinus rhythm. There's a small rise here at P just before the upper heart chambers contract.' She marked it with a cross and labelled it 'P'. 'Then there's the QRS spike…' again, she labelled the points on the trace '…which happens just before the lower heart chambers contract. And finally there's the rise at point T at the end of the beat.'

'To find the number of heartbeats per minute,' Jack added, 'you measure how many big squares there are between the R points—what we call the ''R-R interval''. The ECG machine usually runs at twenty-five millimetres per second so you just divide three hundred by the number of big squares.'

'Some machines run at fifty millimetres per second, so always check if you're not sure,' Miranda added.

Hannah looked at the trace and did a quick calculation. 'Three hundred divided by four—that's seventy-five.'

'Well within the normal resting range,' Miranda pronounced.

She couldn't help looking at Jack. And there was a

distinct question in his eyes which she dared not answer. She forced herself to think of work. 'Do we have a book of sample traces, Jack?'

'For teaching? Yes—I'll go and get it.' He removed the leads. 'You'll be surprised how quickly you learn to spot the differences in the waves and what they mean,' he told Hannah. 'When you first start, you think you'll never remember them all, but you'll soon get the hang of it. And you can always ask one of us if you're not sure. We won't mind or think you're stupid. We've all been in the same position.'

Miranda fiddled with the machine until she heard Jack put his white coat on again. Her face felt hot and she hoped it wasn't too obvious. She could claim that her office was too warm—it was unusually hot for March— but she had a nasty feeling Jack would guess why she was flushed.

She needed to get her professional objectivity back. Fast.

And then she heard the call, 'Crash team!'

'We'll carry on with the traces later,' she told Hannah. 'Come on, we're needed.'

She walked quickly out into the ward and saw the light flashing above the door of Room One. Her heart sank. No. Please, not Imogen, she thought.

Jack was already there, giving CPR at the rate of five chest compressions to one breath, while Leila was getting the defibrillator ready.

'She's in VF,' Leila said. VF, or ventricular fibrillation, was an abnormal heart rhythm—it meant Imogen's heart was contracting quickly but not effectively.

Miranda went straight into action and attached the defibrillator paddles to Imogen's chest so Leila could check the monitor. 'Charging to 360. And clear,' she said. Jack stopped the CPR so Miranda could shock Imogen.

'Still in VF,' Leila said, watching the monitor closely.

'Have you given her adrenaline?' Miranda asked.

'Not yet,' Leila said.

'Hannah, get me some adrenaline now. Charging to 360. And clear,' Miranda repeated. Imogen had to respond. She *had* to. They weren't going to lose her.

'Still in VF,' Leila reported.

'Charging. And clear,' Miranda said.

'She's back in sinus,' Leila said. 'Well done.'

Tears pricked the backs of Miranda's eyes. Thank God. 'Jack, we can't wait until tomorrow morning for the angioplasty. Not now she's had an MI.'

'Bypass?' he asked.

'Yup. I'll call Jordan and sort out a slot in Theatre now. Can you prep her?'

'Will do,' he said.

'Leila, can you get in touch with Emma and tell her that we're taking her great-aunt down to Theatre now, please?' she asked.

'Will do,' Leila said.

'Hannah, check if Leila needs you for anything—if not, you're welcome to come and observe,' Miranda continued.

'Thanks,' Hannah said, flushing faintly.

Miranda rang Jordan and organised an emergency theatre slot. On the way down to Theatre, Imogen arrested again but Jack managed to bring her back. Before Miranda could make the first incision, Imogen arrested again.

'Come on, come *on*,' Jack said. 'We're not letting you go, Imogen. Stay with us. Charging. And clear.'

But this time they couldn't bring her back.

'It's been twenty minutes,' Jack said softly as Miranda continued CPR. 'Do you want me to call it?'

'No. We can't give up now.' She continued giving CPR. 'Come *on*, Imogen. You have to stay with us.'

But it was no use. Gently, Jack put his hands over hers. 'I'm calling it,' he said. 'She's been down too long.'

'No.' Miranda shook her head in frustration. '*No*. We can't have lost her.'

'She's gone,' he said, his voice compassionate yet firm.

Miranda nodded dully, then glanced at the nurse's watch on her white coat. 'Time of death, three twenty-four.' She stroked the old lady's forehead. 'I'm sorry, Imogen. I'm so, so sorry,' she said softly, then turned away. 'I'd better go and ring Emma.' She swallowed hard and walked back to her office to ring Imogen's great-niece.

'But—but she was going to have her operation! I thought she was going to be all right,' Emma said. 'You said you were going to put a balloon in her arteries to clear them, and it would stop her getting the pain any more.'

'I'm so sorry, Emma. We did everything we could. But her heart had just had enough.'

'Poor Imogen. She was… It's *my* fault,' Emma said. 'We should have had her to live with us.'

'It wouldn't have made any difference,' Miranda re-assured her. 'And it wasn't your fault at all. She was ill.'

'I should have done more.'

'You did your best. You came in to see her when you could, and rang when you couldn't—and it isn't easy to care for an elderly relative when you have three small children to look after as well.' Easier if you didn't have children. *She* could have done more for May. But she hadn't, had she?

'I can't believe she's gone.' Emma's voice was unsteady. 'And Floss... I don't know what we're going to do about Floss. We can't have a dog—we're renting and the landlord won't let us have pets, not even a hamster. We can't keep her in kennels but I *can't* have her put down. She's not that old and she's not even ill.'

'I'll see what I can do,' Miranda promised. 'Someone here might be able to give her a new home.'

'Can I...can I come and see my great-aunt?'

'Of course you can. And I'll be here if you want to talk to me.'

'Thank you.' Emma was clearly crying as she rang off.

Miranda returned the receiver to its cradle, put her arms on her desk and rested her head on her arms. If only she'd done the angioplasty the day before. If only...

She heard a click and looked up. Jack had closed her office door. He walked towards her and laid a hand on her shoulder. 'Hey, it's not your fault. It was a risk with anyone who had her condition. You know that.'

'I lost her, Jack.'

'We can't save them all,' he said softly. 'I know how you feel. She was a sweetheart. But she's not in pain any more, and you did your best for her.'

'No, I didn't. I should have told the Prof to stuff his demo and insist on taking my slot back.'

'And she might have arrested on the way down to Theatre yesterday afternoon. Besides, you know the risks with angioplasties. When the balloon inflates and blocks the artery temporarily, that sometimes triggers an MI. The chances were, it would have happened in Imogen's case.' He pulled up a chair next to hers and put his arm round her shoulders. 'Don't blame yourself, Miranda.'

She knew she shouldn't lean towards him. Shouldn't let him hold her. But right then she needed the comfort.

'So what's the real story?' he asked softly. 'We're all upset when we lose a patient—but this really seems to have knocked you for six. You spent time with Imogen when you were supposed to be off duty, and you went and took a photograph of her dog for her. That's going beyond the call of duty.'

Miranda shrugged. 'I liked her.'

'And?'

'I suppose she reminds me of May, my great-aunt.' She hadn't intended to tell Jack any more than that, but somehow the words spilled out. 'May was a cardiac nurse, years ago, and I used to love listening to her stories about the ward. It's one of the reasons I wanted to work in the same area. My father didn't want me to be a cardiologist—he didn't even want me to be a doctor—but May told me to follow my heart and do what I really wanted to do. She said if he cut off my allowance, as he'd threatened, she'd support me through my training.'

Jack whistled. 'I bet that went down well.'

Miranda nodded. 'She was the one who advised me to do my training in Glasgow, away from him—not here. And she was right.'

'And you feel that because we lost Imogen you've let your great-aunt down?'

'Something like that,' she admitted.

'Hey.' He rubbed the pad of his thumb against her cheek. 'She was a medic, too. She knows you try your hardest but you can't save everyone. I bet if you talk to her about it, she'll tell you you're being ridiculous.'

'I wish she could.' Miranda swallowed hard. 'She died two years ago. She—she had unstable angina. She didn't tell any of us, so we had no idea. One day I had a funny feeling. I couldn't get hold of her on the phone, so I dropped in on my way home from work. I had a key—and that's when I found her. She'd had a massive MI. And…' she closed her eyes '…it was too late to do anything.'

He groaned. 'Oh, hell. I'm sorry. No wonder you're so upset. I had no idea. I didn't mean to make things worse.' He leaned forward and kissed away the single tear from her cheek. 'Miranda…'

She wasn't sure which of them moved first. But the next thing she knew, he was kissing her. Really kissing her, his mouth warm and soft and demanding all at the same time. And she was kissing him back, sliding her fingers into his hair and urging him on.

His hands slipped to her waist and he pulled her onto his lap, still kissing her. It was only when she realised that he'd loosened her hair that she pulled back.

'No. We can't do this.'

His pupils had expanded so much his eyes were almost black with desire. His lips were full and slightly swollen, his cheeks were flushed and his hair was a mess. Miranda had a nasty feeling that she looked just as bad. And an even nastier feeling that if she didn't move off his lap right now, she'd end up initiating another kiss. And another. She wanted him to touch her, stroke her skin all over, soothe away her pain with those clever fingers and that beautiful mouth—

No. She had to stop this, right now. With an effort she stood up.

'Miranda, I—' he began.

'I know.' She put her hands behind her back and clenched them together, to stop herself placing a finger on his lips. Stop herself touching him. 'It was unprofessional. But understandable. We were both upset about losing our patient, both wanted comfort—and we were both here.'

'Mmm-hmm.' His mouth was saying he understood. His eyes were saying something entirely different—that he wanted her, and he knew she wanted him, too. It hadn't been just comfort.

'We're colleagues. It wouldn't work out.'

'Mmm-hmm.' Again, his eyes held a different message. *How do we know until we try?*

'And I…' No. She couldn't pull rank on him—even though she *was* his boss, she wasn't going to rub it in that she'd got the job he'd gone for. 'I'm not looking for a relationship.' She might be going out to dinner with Jordan Francis next week, but she'd make very clear to him that it was as friends only. 'My career's the most important thing in my life.'

'Me, too.'

'Good. Then we're agreed—this was a one-off and it didn't mean anything.'

'Yep.'

She dropped her gaze. 'I—um, I'd better sort out the paperwork. And I promised Emma I'd see what I could do about Floss. It's the least I could do for Imogen.' She gave him a quizzical look. 'Do you have a dog?'

'No, and it wouldn't be fair to keep one. Not when I live on my own and work doctors' hours.'

'How about your family?'

'How about yours?' he fenced.

Her mother might, possibly—but her father would definitely refuse. She sighed. 'All right. I'll put a notice on the board in the staffroom and see if anyone wants to take her on.'

'Right. I'd better get cracking on a ward round.'

She couldn't let him walk out of her office looking

like that—not unless she wanted the hospital rumour mill to work overtime! 'You...um, you'd better do something with your hair first,' she said, rummaging in her desk drawer and pulling out a comb.

'Leave yours,' he said softly. 'It's a crime to hide hair that beautiful.'

She flushed, and his body stirred. Hell. They'd just agreed that nothing was going to happen between them. But just looking at her made him want her. Made him remember how her warm, soft mouth had responded to him. How she'd kissed him back.

He was really going to have to keep a tight rein on himself.

'I'll see you at the end of the ward round,' she said. 'Take Hannah with you.'

'Yes, boss.'

She was already pulling her hair back in that severe style. Putting her Ms Brisk-and-Efficient front on. The trouble was, now Jack knew what lay beneath it. And he wanted to know a lot, lot more.

CHAPTER THREE

'So how are you feeling, Sid?' Miranda asked.

'Nervous,' he admitted. 'The wife's been looking things up on the internet. Surgery on what I've got is really risky, isn't it?'

They'd already discussed it before Sid had signed the consent form for the operation, but Miranda had been prepared for last-minute nerves. 'It's risky, yes—but nowhere near as risky as leaving it. If it ruptures—which it's very likely to do, in the next five years—you'll lose a massive amount of blood and you'll only have a fifty per cent chance of making it to hospital. If you do make it, you'll have a fifty per cent chance of coming through the op. That's a one in four chance of surviving.' Miranda squeezed his hand. 'Whereas with surgery you've got an eighty-five to ninety per cent chance of surviving. Better than that, in fact, because that's the average, and Dr Sawyer has plenty of experience. So have I.'

'Bronny says there's something you can do that doesn't mean cutting me open.'

'Keyhole surgery? Yes, but it's still being trialled. There's also something called an endovascular stent, which is a special wire that supports your artery, but again it's experimental. I need to get funding for a trial here before I can do either of them,' Miranda said.

'Can't I wait until you've got the funding?'

She smiled. 'Oh, Sid. I don't know how long it'll take—and I'm not taking any risks with you. If you really, really don't want to have surgery, I'll respect your wishes—but I do think it's in your best interests to have the op.'

'OK, Doc.' Sid looked glum.

'Hey, cheer up. You'll be on your feet again tomorrow and you'll be eating normally in four or five days. And I'll cook you a bacon sandwich myself, to celebrate.'

His smile was watery. 'I'll hold you to that, Doc.'

'It's a deal,' she said. 'No butter—but you can have lots of tomato ketchup.'

'I wish you hadn't said that,' he said. 'I'm starving!'

'I know. But you've got something to look forward to now.'

'And seeing my first grandchild. My Lauren told me yesterday she's expecting.'

'Hey, that's great news. Even better, you're going to be able to play with your grandchild without everyone worrying that you'll keel over.' Miranda squeezed his hand again. 'I know it's hard, but try not to worry, Sid. Claire Barker's going to give you your pre-med, and you'll be out of Theatre before you know it.'

She went to join Jack. 'Ready to scrub?'

'Yep.'

'Miranda?' Claire came over to them, looking worried. 'Sid Patterson's complaining of a pain in his back, between the shoulder blades.'

Jack and Miranda looked at each other. 'Dissection?' Jack asked.

'I don't know what'd be worse, that or a rupture. Claire, is he talking about pain in his chest, arms or stomach?'

'No. He just says he feels a bit funny and his back aches.'

'Let's get him down there now,' Miranda said.

*   *   *

The aneurysm was in the descending part of the aorta, just beneath the heart. 'Fusiform,' Jack commented, seeing the distension all the way round the aorta's circumference, tapering at both ends. 'An absolutely textbook example. The good news is, it hasn't ruptured. I can't see any sign of a tear either—so let's just hope his back pain was due to nerves. Everyone ready?'

'Ready,' the team confirmed.

'OK. On bypass, please.'

Jack worked quickly, clamping the aorta and checking the blood pressure with the anaesthetist and perfusionist. He cut out the damaged part of the blood vessel, then grafted the synthetic material into the artery. Miranda worked flawlessly with him, as if reading his mind— before the words were half out of his mouth she was giving him exactly what he needed.

He was good, she acknowledged. Very good. He'd make an excellent consultant. And, the way things were going between herself and the Prof, that might happen sooner rather than later.

'Ready for clamp removal?' she asked.

He nodded. 'Let's increase the flow rates, see what happens.' He kept a close eye on the suturing. 'Looks as if it's holding up.'

'Release the clamps gradually, please,' Miranda instructed.

They watched the graft area closely as the clamps were released. And then Jack gave a sigh of relief. 'We're there.'

'Want me to close?' Miranda asked.

He nodded. 'Let's leave the double lumen tube in until tomorrow.'

'OK. You go and shower—I'll finish up.'

'Cheers.' He flexed his shoulders. 'Any chance of a back massage as well?'

At least he didn't bear grudges—after he'd stomped out of her office the other day he'd been fine with her. He'd even started bantering with her, the kind of casual, teasing remarks that made her feel as if she'd worked with him for a lifetime instead of just a few days. He was easy to be around. And that, in itself, was dangerous. She couldn't afford to get involved. Even if she hadn't worked with him... No. She'd sworn off relationships for good. Dates were fine—but no commitment. Her judgement in men was lousy, so it was safer to stay on her own. Much safer.

'On your bike, Sawyer,' she informed him with a grin. 'I'll see you back on the ward.'

She stayed with Sid in the post-operative recovery area, then accompanied him back up to the ward.

'It went really well,' she told Bronny Patterson. 'Dr Sawyer did an excellent job. Sid's going to have a tube in his throat for another twenty-four hours to help him breathe and get over the operation, but we'll get him a pen and pad so he can still communicate with you.'

'I don't think anything would stop him communicating,' Bronny said with a smile.

'Bless him.' Miranda echoed her smile. 'He's going to be hooked up to a heart monitor and a blood-pressure monitor, too, and there's a drain in his wound so it doesn't get infected,' she explained. 'I know we went over all this before the op, but sometimes it's hard to take in until you see him, and I don't want you to be frightened by all the tubes and wires. It all went really smoothly, and there's nothing out of the ordinary in his post-operative care.'

'Thanks.'

'Sid told me you'd been doing some research.' Miranda smiled. 'There's some scary stuff out there.'

Bronny nodded. 'I wished I hadn't started when I saw some of the statistics.'

'We'll be keeping a close eye on him. Anyway, I owe him a bacon sandwich. I don't think he'll risk missing that,' Miranda said lightly. 'Or his first grandchild—congratulations, by the way.'

Bronny smiled. 'Thanks.'

'I'll take you through to him now. Is there anything I can get you?'

'No, pet. I'll be fine. But thanks. We both appreciate what you've done.'

'Not me. Dr Sawyer did the hard work.'

'Taking my name in vain?' Jack teased as he met them by the door. But he was oddly pleased all the same. Miranda hadn't known he was there, but she'd still made sure he'd got the credit he was due. It almost made up for the row they'd had after she'd seen the Prof in her office. And even that he could understand now—she'd overreacted because Imogen had reminded her of losing someone she'd loved dearly.

'Thank you, Dr Sawyer,' Bronny said, taking his hand and squeezing it.

'No problem,' he said with a smile. He waited until Bronny was settled in with Sid, then caught Miranda on her way out of the room. 'I'll stay here tonight,' he said. 'Just in case.'

'You will not,' she informed him. 'You're off duty and I have the bleeper.'

'But—'

'Plus I'm expecting you in the Calderford Arms,' she

added. 'When I said I'd buy everyone on the ward a drink, I meant everyone.'

'What about the night staff?' he fenced.

'That's covered, too. I've left them a stack of nibbles and some decent soft drinks.' She eased her shoulders. 'We've had a rough week. I think we all need to let our hair down. I'm taking my bleeper and my mobile, so I can get back here quickly if I'm needed.' She smiled at him. 'Go and get your glad rags on.'

'Yes, boss.' He could just see it now. The rest of the staff would be dressed up to the nines, but she'd still be wearing her formal business suit, with her hair scraped back.

'See you there. Seven o'clock sharp.'

'I'll be there,' he promised. 'Though I hope you're not going to start doing paperwork now.'

She gave him another of those smiles that clearly said, *Don't ask questions.* 'See you in the Calderford Arms.'

When she strolled into the bar at precisely seven o'clock, Leila dug Jack in the ribs. 'Close your mouth,' she said.

'Uh,' was all Jack could say. Because Ms Fluffy was back—and how! Her hair was loose and fell over her shoulders in glossy waves. She wasn't wearing much make-up—no more than a light slick of lip-gloss and a coat of mascara—but it was her clothing that really floored Jack. A crop top which revealed a smooth, flat torso, a pair of black trousers that were slung low round her hips, high-heeled strappy shoes and what he had a nasty feeling was a real diamond in her navel.

She looked a million dollars. And the desire he'd felt for her when he'd kissed her in her office was suddenly magnified a thousandfold.

'Evening, all,' she said. Still in her posh voice. Still as

if she were on the ward. It was like having double vision, he thought. Or as if his audio and visual systems weren't working in synch. She *sounded* like the efficient doctor he'd worked with for the past week—but she *looked* like a bad boy's wildest dream.

'What are you having?' she asked.

You, please. Just you, Jack thought. Then he got a grip on himself. Just. 'Orange juice, please.'

She narrowed her eyes. 'You're not going back to the hospital tonight—I've already told you, I'm checking on Sid later. So if you want a beer or whatever, that's fine.'

'Orange juice,' he repeated with a smile.

'OK.' She took everyone's order, got the first round in, then announced that when everyone had finished there was another of the same lined up for them.

Jack watched her work the room. She spent time with everyone and, from the snatches of conversation he heard, either she'd known most of these people for years or she'd really done her homework with their personnel files. Whichever it was, she sounded genuinely interested in her colleagues. Even the quieter nurses responded well to her, chatting as if they were lifelong friends.

He'd done some homework himself after that kiss. And discovered that she'd really meant it about her career. Friends in Glasgow had been quick to tell him that Miranda Turner had a reputation for being untouchable. She dated—lots—but no one lasted more than two dates. And no one ever got past first base with her.

Not that it was any of his business what she did. Even if they hadn't been working on the same ward—if she hadn't been his boss—it could never work between them. They were worlds apart. And yet there was something about her. Something that made him want to break all his personal rules, and then some.

'Hey. Just because you performed a difficult major op this afternoon—with a great deal of finesse, I might add—it doesn't give you the right to sit there with a long face. What's up?'

He had to drag his eyes away from that damned navel ring. 'Nothing.'

'Then give me a smile, Jack. No, a proper one.' She rolled her eyes. 'OK. So you disapprove of the navel ring.'

Not disapprove, exactly. 'It's…not what I expected.'

She grinned. 'Because I'm too sensible? Or too prim and proper?'

'Both,' he admitted. Hell, was it that obvious what he thought of her?

'Sometimes you need to let your hair down.'

Oh, yes. Just like Jessica. Out for a good time.

'Isn't there a saying about you? All work and no play makes Jack a dull boy?'

'I can play with the best of them,' he retorted, stung. Then he saw the look in her eyes. Was it his imagination, or were they daring him? No, it had to be his imagination. He was seeing what he wanted to see. Awareness. Interest. Desire.

And he really, really had to stop thinking about that kiss.

'Then you're coming to Louie's with us?'

Louie's was a Creole restaurant in the centre of Calderford, with a dance-floor right in the middle of it. 'Food or dancing?'

'Both. I'm getting one more round in first.'

No, it wasn't his imagination. Her eyes were definitely daring him. Miranda was in the mood to play. Right, so was he. 'I'm up for it if you are,' he said softly, then moistened his lower lip. And then he had the satisfaction of seeing the slightest flush stain her cheekbones.

Miranda, being typically efficient, had organised taxis to take everyone into the centre of Calderford. Jack found himself sitting next to her in the taxi, and it took all his strength to resist taking her hand and curling his fingers round hers. They'd already agreed that nothing was going to happen between them—so why wasn't his body listening?

It got worse when they reached Louie's because he was at the same table as Miranda. And although he could have sworn she was sticking to mineral water—she had to be, she was on call—everyone else was slightly tipsy, and she was joining in the fun as if she'd been drinking, too. To the point of scoffing at the plain chicken he'd ordered and insisting that he try a mouthful of her shrimp and okra gumbo.

'It's spicy, yes, but the chilli's there for sweetness, not heat,' she said. 'Come on, you haven't lived until you've tried this.'

When she held the fork to his lips, what else could he do but try it? But then he started imagining her feeding him delicacies, morsel by morsel, when they were alone. Undisturbed. And… No. He had to stop thinking about that—right now.

'Well?' she asked.

'It's better than I expected,' he admitted.

She grinned. 'C'mon. Seafood and veg. You're a cardiologist. You know they're good for you.'

'And I suppose that's "fruit"?' he asked when her pudding arrived.

'Strawberries,' she said, laughing.

'And doughnuts,' he said. 'Which *don't* count.'

'Beignets, actually.' She broke off a piece and held it

to his mouth. 'They're made with yeast but cooked before the dough gets a chance to rise.'

Trust her to know exactly how they were cooked. But he had to admit they were good. The fact she'd hand-fed him… No. No. He wasn't going to let his thoughts go down that track.

'So you've been to Louie's a lot?' he asked.

'There's a branch in Glasgow,' she said. 'Most hospital parties end up there. The food's good and so's the music.'

'So you can actually do Creole dancing?' The words were out before he could stop them.

'It's called Zydeco.' She gave him an impish look. 'Are you telling me you can't?'

'I don't do dancing.'

It was completely the wrong thing to say. Because she pulled him to his feet. 'Time you learned, then.'

'Miranda—'

'After the week I've had,' she said softly, 'I need this.'

His mouth dried. Was she saying she wanted him? But…she'd been the one to break that kiss. Had she changed her mind?

Just like Jessica, he thought bitterly. Wanting him one minute, cool with him the next. He'd sworn he'd never be in that position again. He'd never let another woman make him her plaything, her 'bit of rough'—fun for now but thrown over as soon as a better offer came along. And that included Miranda Turner.

'I'd rather sit it out, thanks all the same,' he said stiffly.

She refused to let go of his hands. 'I'm not planning to make a fool of you, Jack.'

His eyes narrowed. What did she know about his past? But, no, she couldn't know about Jessica. Unless… A sick feeling settled in the pit of his stomach. Had she been one of Jessica's set? Had she been one of the girls who'd laughed at him years before? He couldn't remember her. But it had been a long time ago, people changed a lot between their teens and mid-twenties. And she must be around his age, in her early thirties. She probably looked completely different now.

Or maybe he was prejudging her. Maybe she hadn't been part of Jessica's set. Maybe she just meant she wasn't going to let him look stupid on the dance-floor.

'Dance with me. Please?'

He ought to refuse her. But he found himself letting him lead him onto the dance-floor.

'It's easier to dance together in the close position,' she said, moving so that his feet were between hers. 'Put your left hand on my shoulder and just follow what I'm doing.' Her right hand slid round his back, pulling him close. Close enough for him to smell her perfume.

She guided him through the steps. And then her fingers curled round his and lifted his right hand high up, and she leaned in to him a little more, moving closer. If his life had depended on it, he couldn't have moved away.

'You're a quick learner. Natural rhythm,' she said approvingly.

Rhythm. He wished she hadn't said that word. It sent all sorts of ideas spinning through his mind—he just hoped she couldn't feel how his heartbeat had suddenly gone erratic. He forced himself to make neutral conversation. 'So how come you dance so well?'

'Because I hate sport and no way am I going to set foot in a gym. Swimming's tedious and this is a much more fun way to stay in shape.'

And what a shape. He couldn't resist dropping his hand from her shoulder, sliding it down her back to the base of her spine. The softness of her skin against his fingertips was driving him crazy. It was just as well they were in a public place, or he'd start doing something they'd both regret later. 'I need to know,' he murmured in her ear, just resisting the temptation to brush her earlobe with his lips. 'Is that a *real* diamond in your belly button?'

'Yep. Half of my twenty-first birthday present from my parents.'

Well, that figured. Of course she'd had a hugely expensive present from her parents. She'd probably had driving lessons for her seventeenth and a car for her eighteenth, not to mention a huge party. His own twenty-first had been much more low-key, though his mother and brothers had saved up to buy him some textbooks he'd needed but hadn't been able to afford.

'I had it reset.'

His brain really wasn't working properly. Not when she was close like this. It took most of his concentration to stop himself kissing her. She'd had the diamond reset? 'Are you saying…?'

'I did the teenage rebel thing a bit late,' she said with a grin that made him want to show her exactly what being a rebel meant. 'It was my graduation present to me. Dad blew a fuse when he found out that I'd had my belly button pierced.'

'I think our patients would, too,' he murmured. 'If you go onto the ward dressed like this…'

'I'll put my white coat on over the top and button it up. No one'll know.'

He'd know. And the knowledge was going to give him some difficult moments next time he saw her at work. He'd think of her as she was now. In his arms. Holding him close. Her scent. The feel of her skin against his…

Dancing with Jack like this was dangerous. Crazy. Mad. Especially after they'd shared that kiss in her office. It

wasn't even as if she could blame it on too much wine—
she was on call, so she wasn't drinking. What on earth
had possessed her to tease him into dancing with her?
Especially Zydeco dancing, where the heat between partners rose with the fast, pounding beat.

But it felt good—the slight pressure between their
raised hands, the way he was holding her close, the firm-
ness of the muscles in his back beneath her fingers. And
the music suited him: dark and intense. Like his eyes.

She looked up, and immediately wished she hadn't
given in to the impulse to meet his gaze. Because it reminded her too much of that moment in her office. The
moment when he'd kissed her and loosened her hair.

As if he'd read her mind, he said, 'Your hair looks
beautiful like that. Like one of those lush Rossetti pictures.' His voice was husky, pitched low with desire…or
was that just her own desire she could hear? 'I can just
imagine you draped in blue silk, holding a pomegranate.'

Hell. Now she could imagine it, too. Blue silk that she
could let drift to the floor, so he could—No. Stop right
there, she told herself. 'Not practical for work,' she muttered.

'The pomegranate or the hair?'

'Both.' And this was her get-out. She seized it gratefully. 'And, talking of work, I really ought to pop back
and see how Sid is.'

'I'll come with you,' he offered.

She shook her head. 'Stay and enjoy the dancing. I've
put some money behind the bar for another round—tell
the others for me.'

'I will—and thanks—but I really don't think it's a
good idea to go off on your own on a Friday night in the
middle of Calderford.'

He didn't add 'dressed like that', but she knew that was what he meant.

'I'll be perfectly safe in a taxi. And I did a course in self-defence when I was a student. I can look after myself, Jack.' Right then she trusted the roughest part of Calderford more than she trusted herself. She needed distance between herself and Jack—and she needed it now, before she did something stupid. Like cupping his face in her hands and drawing his mouth down to hers. Like kissing him until they were both dizzy. Like asking him to take her home, make her forget the horrors of the week.

'If you insist. But I'm waiting with you until the taxi arrives,' he warned.

To her relief, the spell seemed to break once they were away from the music. If Jack noticed, he didn't say anything. He merely joined her in shop talk until the taxi arrived, and told her to call him if she needed a hand.

All I really need, she thought as the taxi drove away, is a large dose of common sense. And to focus on my goal: my career. First, last and always.

CHAPTER FOUR

'YOU'RE supposed to be off duty,' Jack remarked.

'Huh?' Miranda stopped typing and looked up from the computer to see him leaning against her office doorway.

'Off duty,' he repeated.

'Oh. That.' She waved a hand dismissively. 'I just popped in to see how Sid was and make sure he's managed to get on his feet today.'

'As the duty doctor, I'm perfectly capable of doing that.'

'I know, and I wasn't checking up on you.'

He believed her. She'd been in to see Sid on Saturday as well. This wasn't about trusting him—this was because she lived for her work. 'You just worry about your patients, hmm?'

She smiled and his heart kicked. Hell. He'd promised himself he was going to concentrate on his career—that he wasn't going to start even looking for Ms Right until he'd made consultant. That smile made him think maybe that was a mistake. Maybe he should be looking at Ms Right-In-Front-Of-His-Nose instead. Though he'd already gone through a dozen reasons why he shouldn't get involved with her.

Then he became aware that she was looking at him. 'Sorry. I didn't quite catch what you said.' He hoped she hadn't guessed why.

'Just that you were right. I worry about my patients.'

'Well, you've seen Sid twice, this weekend. Half a

glance at his notes would tell you that he's doing fine. So why are you in your office right now?'

'Just working on an idea.' She shrugged, clearly trying to be laid-back, then sighed. 'Oh, all right. You might as well know, because I want to run it by you anyway when I've done the first draft. I'm working up a research proposal for trialling endovascular stents and keyhole surgery on aneurysms.'

And she was so dedicated to her career that she was writing the proposal on her day off. Shouldn't that be enough to warn him off—to tell him that she wasn't interested in a relationship with anyone, let alone him? 'Right.' He glanced at his watch. And he couldn't resist asking, 'Want to have lunch with me and talk about it?'

There wasn't any evidence of the heat in Jack's eyes that she'd seen on Friday night. The offer had been purely that of a colleague. They were going to discuss work. And that feeling of disappointment was…ridiculous, she told herself. They'd already agreed, they were colleagues only. And tomorrow night she was supposed to be going out with Jordan Francis, so she shouldn't be thinking of other men anyway.

Thanks, but I'm busy, her mouth should have said. It turned traitor and smiled at him instead. 'Yes, why not?'

'Great. See you back here in half an hour.'

'OK.' Miranda made the mistake of watching him walk away. And instead of seeing the dedicated young doctor in sober black trousers, white shirt, discreet tie and white coat, she saw him as he'd been at the restaurant when they'd danced together. Wearing stone-coloured chinos and a black round-necked cotton sweater. He'd looked fabulous, and she knew that every pair of female eyes around the dance-floor had been concentrating on him.

'You don't do relationships, you don't date men on your own ward—especially when you're their senior—and you're supposed to be focusing on your career,' she reminded herself quietly.

She continued working on her proposal, and it felt more like five seconds than thirty minutes later when Jack returned to collect her for lunch.

'I still can't believe you're wasting a day like this,' Jack said, gesturing to the bright blue spring sky. 'You could be at the beach, strolling through the park.' No. Bad move—because he could imagine himself there by her side. Just holding her hand. Well, maybe not. Maybe an arm round her shoulders. Round her waist. Holding her close. Kissing...

His mouth went dry and he had to swallow hard. 'And yet you're stuck in here,' he finished. 'Why?'

'I just wanted to start my proposal.'

Work clearly came first with her. 'You really are ambitious, aren't you?'

Miranda nodded. 'And I'm prepared to put the hours in to get where I want to be.'

She hadn't needed to tell him that. He'd already seen it for himself. She was as dedicated as he was—probably more so. Now he was beginning to see just why she'd got the job. As well as ability, she had dedication. In spades. 'You're already consultant. What next? Your father's job?'

'No. I was thinking more a research fellowship somewhere. Half teaching, half working with patients. That way, I get to do some blue-sky work and push the boundaries of medical knowledge just that little bit further but

I don't get stuck in an ivory tower. I don't want to end up forgetting that my job's to help people get better, not just to see how clever I am and what wonderful theories I can dream up.'

He could imagine her doing it, too. He could imagine her winning the Nobel Prize. But in ten, twenty years' time...what then? Would she still be concentrating on her career? Or was there a place in her plans for a family?

He only just stopped himself asking her. It was none of his business. Besides, he knew from his experience with Jessica that women like Miranda wouldn't see him as serious relationship material. And he didn't want to be just a bit of fun. 'Sounds good.'

'Is that what you're looking for, too?'

A family? No, of course not. She meant *work*. 'No. I'm aiming for clinical director. Except I want to make it more a hands-on role.'

'Well, at least we're not going to be competing for the same job in future,' she said wryly.

'Just think. In a few years' time, I could be clinical director here, and you could be professor at Calderford University.'

'That's scary. Anyway, haven't you thought about moving away from Calderford to take the next step up? It'd give you more opportunities.'

'Yes—but my mother would drive me bananas. At least if I live in the same city, she'll give me space.'

Miranda frowned. 'I'm not with you.'

'She likes to know what I'm up to. If she thinks I'm too far away, she'll be on the phone several times a day,' he explained, then grimaced. 'That sounds bad. I don't mean that I don't love her. Of course I do. Just that...sometimes I need space.' And not being nagged about when he was going to settle down, or told what a fantastic father he'd make, or asked when he was going to bring one of his girlfriends to his family Sunday afternoons. Yet he owed his mother way too much to hurt her by moving away.

'Yeah.'

She looked as if she understood. Then he caught a slight flash of panic in her eyes. What had he said?

'D'you know, the blossom on the ground over there looks as if the car park's been turned to coconut ice.'

Somehow he'd spooked her into changing the subject. He decided to let it go. 'Very poetic.'

'Do you always get this grumpy when you're hungry?'

He laughed. 'I think I'm beginning to like you.' Think? Knew. And there was no 'beginning' about it—he liked her a *lot*.

'Good. Otherwise you'd just have to lump me.'

'Because you're not changing for anyone.'

'Got it in one.'

They were both smiling when they joined the lunchtime queue.

But Jack's smile vanished completely a few moments later when Jordan Francis joined the queue behind her. 'Hey, Miranda!' He put his arm round her shoulders and gave Jack a look that said quite clearly, Hands off, she's mine. 'I didn't know you were in today.'

'Just doing some research,' she said.

'You should have said. We could have had lunch together.'

She gave him a sweet smile. 'I'm having lunch with Jack.'

'And you're going to talk shop. OK. I get the hint.' He squeezed her shoulders. 'Though promise me tomorrow night we're not going to even mention the hospital.'

'Sure.'

Tomorrow night? Jack didn't like the sound of that. Please, no. Somebody tell him she wasn't really going out with the theatre manager. 'What's this, a hot date or something?' Jack asked, hoping his voice sounded a lot more casual than he felt.

'That's right.' Jordan threw him a challenging look.

Miranda groaned inwardly as she saw the look on both their faces. Oh, no. She wasn't having a male competition starting up over her. 'As friends,' she said. 'Just like you and I are having lunch *as friends*, Jack.'

Jordan gave her a hurt look. 'But I thought—'

'We're having dinner together,' she said, this time more gently. 'And we'll be going Dutch. I don't expect my friends to pay for me.'

'I see.'

Oh, hell. She really should have made it clearer when she'd accepted his invitation. Dinner out was fine, but she wasn't in the market for a relationship. 'Jordan,' she said softly, 'we'll talk about this tomorrow night, OK?'

'OK,' he said, but he still looked crestfallen.

'I don't see why you're going out with him,' Jack commented, when they'd chosen their food and found a table—a table which Jordan noticeably chose the table furthest away from. 'You do know he tries it on with every girl he goes out with, don't you?'

'And you do realise that I'm a big girl and perfectly capable of looking after myself?' she flashed back.

Colour slid over his cheekbones. 'No need to be snippy.'

'I choose my own friends, Jack. Tomorrow night I'm going out for dinner with Jordan. And I'm going to have a good time. OK?'

'Fine,' he said tightly.

'You know,' she said, 'if you want to make it to clin-

ical director level, you're going to have to work on your
social skills.'

'I beg your pardon?'

'Social skills,' she repeated. 'You have to be able to
talk to anyone—be friendly.'

His eyes narrowed. 'You're telling me to schmooze?'

'No. Just that you have to find something in common
with people you deal with, something to let you get on
with them. And don't stereotype them. A posh accent
doesn't necessarily mean someone's pulled strings to get
the job. You're going to have to get over that chip on
your shoulder.'

'I haven't got a chip on my shoulder!' he said, outraged.

'You had one about me.'

'Which was entirely reasonable, in the circumstances.'

'No, it wasn't. You made your judgement before you
knew all the facts. You need to learn to hold back a bit
and listen, not jump straight in.'

'Says the woman who jumped straight in and had a go
at the Prof.'

She flinched. 'Thanks for bringing that up.'

'You're the one who believes in straight talking.'

'I do. But you need to be able to do social niceties as
well—and know when to be pleasant and when to be
straight. Now, do you want to know about this proposal
or not?'

'OK, boss,' he drawled. She pulled a face at him, then
took a printout from her handbag and started talking him
through her proposal.

The following day, Jack was forced to acknowledge that,
yes, he was jealous of Jordan Francis. Even though he
knew that Jordan wouldn't get more than a second date

from Miranda—who was going out with him on a friends-only basis anyway—the idea of another man going out with Miranda unsettled him. Annoyed him. Downright *irritated* him.

Worse, he couldn't tell her that. If he told Miranda his professional reservations about Jordan Francis, she'd only think he was jealous. They'd managed to establish a decent working relationship and he didn't want to spoil that. Besides, she'd already told him that she was concentrating on her career. Hell, she'd even told him her career plan—a plan that most definitely didn't include a relationship. She hadn't once mentioned the words husband, marriage or even family.

She hadn't even said much to him today—just done the ward round then given him a copy of her research proposal and asked him to let her know his thoughts by end of play Wednesday as she was having lunch with the Prof to discuss it on Friday.

He pulled a face. Huh. It was just the Monday blues. Nothing to do with Miranda Turner. Nothing to do with that navel ring and the way she'd danced with him on Friday night, her body warm and soft and close to his...

'Got a minute?' the object of his thoughts asked, leaning round the door to his office.

'Er—sure.'

'What do you know about Eisenmenger syndrome?'

He thought about it. 'The pressure of the blood circulating in the pulmonary arteries is very high and the pressure on the right side of the heart is higher than the left, so the blood flow reverses. Deoxygenated blood mixes with oxygenated blood and the patient has a blue tinge to his skin, especially around the lips and fingertips.' The colouring was known as cyanosis.

She nodded. 'Other symptoms?'

'Breathlessness, fatigue, loud second heart sound, often a murmur such as a Graham Steell—which is high-pitched, louder when the patient breathes in and gradually gets quieter. The patient's red blood cells increase—if levels get to more than twenty grams per decilitre, the blood gets sticky and the patient may get a headache and find it hard to concentrate. Oh, and there's an increased risk of stroke, from the sticky blood and from air bubbles in the right-to-left shunt. And the patient's more likely to suffer from gallstones and gout.'

'OK, Sawyer, you pass your viva,' she said with a grin.

'We haven't any regulars with Eisenmenger's,' he said thoughtfully. 'Have we just had an admission?'

'Not yet. It's a three-month check-up—Dan Lowe's just moved to the area and his GP thought he'd better book him in to see us. He's coming in this afternoon.'

'How old is he?' Jack asked.

'Twenty-five.'

Jack nodded. Patients with Eisenmenger syndrome were lucky to reach thirty. 'Hole in the heart when he was born?' It was the most common cause of the syndrome.

Miranda nodded. 'VSD.' VSD or ventricular septal defect meant there was a hole between the two ventricles or pumping chambers of the heart. 'It was repaired, but Eisenmenger's was diagnosed when he was twelve.'

'No transplant matches yet?' The main cure was a heart-lung transplant, though just a lung transplant was a possibility in some cases.

'Apparently not. We haven't had the notes through from his old hospital yet either.' She rolled her eyes. 'So the poor guy's going to need the works. Full blood count, biochemical profile, iron studies, blood gases, ECG and echo. I think we should let Hannah sit in on this, too.'

'It'd be good experience for her,' he agreed.

'He's booked in for half-two. See you then.'

Which made it clear she had other plans for lunch. Fine. He couldn't monopolise her. Didn't want to either.

Jack pulled a face. And just who was he trying to kid?

Dan Lowe was the quiet, studious type. Not that he could have been the athletic kind—patients with Eisenmenger's had to avoid strenuous exercise, which could give them a heart arrhythmia or reduce their oxygen saturation levels too much.

Miranda introduced herself to him. 'And these are my colleagues, Jack Sawyer and Hannah Perry.'

'Pleased to meet you,' Dan said.

'We'd like to give you a few tests so we can see your condition properly. I imagine you're as familiar with the tests as we are, but if you don't understand why we're doing anything, just stop us and ask,' Miranda said. 'Hannah will take blood samples and do your ECG and echo, and then we can have a bit of a chat.'

'That's fine,' he said.

When Hannah had finished doing the tests, Miranda asked Dan, 'So what brought you to Calderford?'

'Promotion. I'm an accountant,' he said quietly. 'The firm gave me a chance to become team leader up here. It meant moving from Suffolk, but I wanted to get on.'

'Good for you,' she said. 'So how have you been feeling?'

'Fine.'

'Any dizziness or headaches?' Jack asked.

'No.'

'Bruising or coughing up blood?' Miranda asked.

'No.'

'How about your heart?' Jack asked.

Dan shrugged. 'Normal.'

'Normal normal, or normal for you?' Miranda asked.

He smiled. 'Normal normal—I think.'

'Any funny little flutters, any aches or pains?' she checked.

'None.'

'Good—you're doing well.' Miranda listened to his heart. As she'd expected, there was a loud second heart sound, plus a murmur. The ECG had shown the wave abnormalities she was expecting, but at least his blood tests showed that everything was in the normal range for a patient with Dan's condition.

'So I take it you already know all about the importance of not overdoing it with exercise, but doing some daily stretching and walking,' Miranda said.

'Oh, yes.' Dan gave her a rueful smile. 'And stay out of saunas and hot tubs, and forget having long hot showers in case any of them make my blood pressure drop too much.'

'Wow—model patient!' Miranda grinned at him. 'Smoking, alcohol and salt?'

'No, no and moderate. I'm keeping to my correct weight. And, no, I don't do recreational drugs either, or work in extreme temperatures.' Dan gave her a sidelong look. 'And I suppose climbing K2 next week is out?'

'So's the Cresta Run, kick-boxing and running that marathon through the desert,' she joked back. 'And you're keeping your fluid levels up?'

He nodded.

'Excellent. Hannah, how would you tell Dan to avoid endocarditis?' she asked.

'Um—to make sure you don't get an infection in the lining of your heart or heart valves, you need to visit your dentist regularly, brush your teeth twice a day with a soft-bristled brush, don't bite your nails and don't use anything abrasive on your skin,' the student recited.

'Well done,' Miranda said softly.

'What about a razor?' Dan asked. 'Or should I grow one of those Robinson Crusoe beards?'

Miranda knew he was teasing and shook her head gravely. 'I dunno. The quiet ones always turn out to be the worst, don't they, Jack?'

'So I pass muster?' Dan asked.

She nodded. 'You're doing really well right now, but you know at some point you're going to need a heart-lung transplant.'

'Yeah. I hated it when I was a kid—all the restrictions—but if it's a case of keeping well or dropping down dead in the middle of the street…' He shrugged. 'There isn't much choice.'

'I know. And you're doing all the right things. Come back and see me in three months. Though if you're feeling unwell at all before then—any feeling of breathlessness, any pain, any coughing up blood or headaches—ring me and I'll see you straight away.'

'Thanks, Doc.'

'Any time. I'll check the transplant lists and see how things are going. The second I hear anything, I'll be in touch.'

'Why does it always happen to the nice ones?' Hannah asked when Dan had left.

'I can't answer that,' Miranda said. 'But we're doing our best for him.'

'And even five years ago survival rates weren't as good as they are now,' Jack said. 'Medicine moves on. Every day we get a bit closer to finding the cures we want.'

'I know. I just hate…well, knowing that we can't save everyone.'

'Hey.' Jack patted her shoulder. 'Come on, pet. I'll shout you a coffee. You, too, Miranda.'

'Sorry—another patient to see,' she said. 'But thanks for the offer.'

She still hadn't quite got Jack out of her head when she met Jordan at Firenze, the Italian restaurant a couple of streets from where she lived.

'Thanks for booking this.' She kissed him lightly on the cheek.

'Pleasure.' Jordan escorted her into the restaurant, made sure that a waiter took her jacket and then held her chair out for her.

Old-fashioned good manners. Miranda liked that. But she needed to get something cleared up. Fast.

'Jordan, there isn't a nice way of putting this,' she said quietly. 'It's not you—not at all. But I've only been in this job for a week, and I need to make that my priority. I can't even start to think about having a relationship other than just friends. I'm sorry if I led you to expect anything else.'

'Fair enough.' He smiled. 'Just as long as you don't think I asked you out to curry favour with the Prof.'

'No, not at all.' She might have lousy judgement in men, but she'd learned the hard way to see through that one. And she wasn't going to let herself get in that position again—or repeat what had happened with Rupert. 'So we understand each other?'

'Yes.' He smiled wryly. 'It doesn't stop me fancying you. But I respect that you just want to be friends.'

'Thanks. I don't have time for a relationship right now.'

Liar, her heart said. You'd make the time if it was a certain someone else. Except they'd already agreed it wouldn't work. So there was no point in thinking of might-have-beens.

'Anything wrong?' Jordan asked. 'You looked a bit…well, upset.'

'Just thinking. Um—do you have a dog?'

'No, and my landlord won't let me. Why?'

'I lost a patient last week. Her family can't take on her dog.' Miranda sighed. 'And I… Well, I promised to find Floss a home.'

'I could try the theatre nurses for you,' Jordan offered.

'Thanks.' Miranda started to feel guilty. Jordan was a genuinely nice bloke—even if Jack *did* think the guy had a bad reputation. And she'd agreed to go out with him tonight. So the very least she could do was concentrate on him and keep Jack Sawyer out of her head.

Though that was easier said than done.

CHAPTER FIVE

'OH, I could *kiss* you!'

Jack stopped dead in the corridor. Miranda wanted to kiss someone? Who? None of your business, he reminded himself. But he couldn't stop himself listening. He really, really had to know who she was talking to—who was making her give that delicious gurgle of laughter.

'OK. I'll meet you there at five. OK. Bye, Jordan.'

Jordan Francis? Jack fought the surge of mingled dismay and anger. She only dated men twice, didn't she? This was a second date, which meant the end of Jordan Francis. Or was it? Had she enjoyed herself so much last night that she'd changed her mind about relationships? No, no, no. She couldn't. Jordan wasn't the right one for her. It would be—

'Did you want something?'

He promptly dropped the notes he was holding. 'Sorry. Didn't see you there,' he muttered as he scrabbled on the floor. Damn. When had she come out of her office? How long had he been standing there, wool-gathering?

She grinned as she helped him pick up the papers. 'You're away with the fairies today.'

'Yeah. Sorry.'

'Hey, I've got some good news. We've found a home for Floss.'

'Imogen's Westie?'

'Yep. Jordan asked around the theatre nurses for me this morning. Sadie's mum lost her Jack Russell last week and she's happy to take Floss on. I'm meeting him with Sadie at Berrybank tonight.'

So it wasn't a date? Jack nearly sagged in relief. 'That's good,' he said, trying to keep his voice light. What he really wanted to do was punch the air and cheer. And that unnerved him even more—he wasn't in the market for a relationship. Particularly with Miranda Turner. He just had to keep reminding himself of that.

Though it was easier said than done. Later that afternoon he smelt bacon. He followed his nose—and found Miranda in Sid's room.

'You've got to work for this, Sidney Patterson,' she said firmly. 'If you want the sandwich, then you walk over here.'

'I can't.'

'Yes, you can. One step at a time.' She glanced at the distance between them. 'I make it half a dozen steps to this chair—eight, tops. You can do it. Come on.'

'You're a hard woman,' he complained. 'You should've been one of those matrons.'

'Oh, I'm much scarier than a matron,' she told him with a grin. 'Come on, Sid. I promised you a bacon sandwich, and here it is.'

'You didn't tell me there were strings attached,' he grumbled.

'I made the bread myself, too. Fresh, home-made granary bread,' she said temptingly. 'And think of that nice grilled bacon. Can't you smell how good it'll taste? Or do Bronny and I have to go shares in your sandwich as well as our own?'

'You know she's right,' Sid's wife said, smiling.

'Horrible woman. And I mean both of you,' he grumbled, but finally he allowed Bronny to help him to his feet. And he walked over to the chair. Very, very slowly—but he did it.

'Well done, you.' Miranda handed him the plate. 'Sid, you really don't have to panic. Yes, you've had a major operation, but you're not going to burst your stitches just by moving. You need to take gentle exercise and gradually increase the amount every day until you're walking for a good thirty minutes, three times a week.'

'You'll have me running a marathon next.'

She grinned. 'If you ever decide to do that, I'll sponsor you.'

'And so will I,' Jack said from the doorway. 'I smell bacon.'

Miranda groaned. 'Wait for it. He's going to claim he deserves a sandwich, too. Because he's a hard-working doctor.'

'I missed breakfast,' he deadpanned.

'Then set your alarm five minutes earlier.' She rolled her eyes. 'All right. I'll share mine with you.' She handed him half her sandwich.

He couldn't help asking, 'Did you really make the bread?' She wasn't the domesticated type—was she?

She gave him a look that said very clearly, *Just how long were you standing there?* 'Yes.'

He took a bite. 'Mmm. Not bad. Count me in for that marathon, if this is what I'll get at the end of it.' Though he'd run in record time if she was waiting for him at the finish line—waiting to hold him close.

Stop right there and concentrate on your sandwich, he told himself. Your patients. Anything—just stop thinking about her.

On Wednesday, Claire Barker came round with a collection for their ward auxiliary's wedding present.

'Of course I'll contribute,' Miranda said. She opened her desk drawer and frowned. She was sure she'd left her handbag zipped up.

'Oh, hell,' she said when she opened her purse. It was completely empty.

'What's up?' Claire asked.

'It's my own fault—I should have locked my handbag in the safe. Or at least locked it in my desk drawer.' She bit her lip. 'It was an open invitation to a sneak thief.'

'You'd better report it,' Claire said. 'Anything else gone, or just the money?'

'My cards are still here,' Miranda said, inspecting her purse. 'And my driving licence.' She breathed out in relief. 'At least I don't have to spend ages on the phone to various officials cancelling everything. I'll give you some money this afternoon, when I've had a chance to get some cash, OK?'

'Thanks. But make sure you tell Security,' Claire said.

'I will, though it's probably a one-off, someone just taking an opportunity. We all know this sort of thing happens in hospitals,' Miranda said. 'Though it's easy to forget and stop taking proper care. Maybe I'd better stick a note in the staff restroom to remind everyone to keep their belongings locked away.' She continued to rummage through her bag, and let out a small cry of anguish. 'Oh, no.'

'What?'

She swallowed hard. 'My great-aunt's nursing watch.'

'It meant a lot to you?' Claire guessed.

'Yeah.' More than a lot. May had given it to her just before her finals, as a lucky charm. And Miranda had carried it around with her ever since. Usually, she pinned it to her white coat, but today she'd had a meeting first so she'd left it in her bag. And it had been taken. It was gone. Her precious memory of May.

'I'm sorry.'

'Not your fault.' She dug her fingernails into the palm of her hand. There was nothing she could do about it, so what was the point in crying? It wouldn't bring the watch back. She had no idea who'd taken it—no idea even when it had been stolen. 'I'll get on to Security.'

When Jack came on duty a couple of hours later, he read Miranda's note and went straight to her office. 'What's happened?' he asked.

She told him about the money.

'And?'

'What do you mean, and?'

'You don't strike me as the type who'd be bothered by money.'

She sighed. 'Whoever it was took my great-aunt's nursing watch from my bag.'

'Your great-aunt May?'

'Yes.'

'Oh, Miranda.'

She shrugged. 'I'll live.'

'You sure you're OK?'

'I'm fine,' she said tightly.

'If I'd lost something that meant a lot to me—even if it wasn't worth a lot in cash terms—I'd need a hug,' he said. 'Come here.'

She did want a hug. Badly. But if Jack touched her…she had a nasty feeling she'd start crying. Not to mention the fact that his touch did strange things to her composure anyway. 'I said I was fine,' she informed him, pulling away before he could touch her.

He lifted his hands in surrender. 'Suit yourself,' he said.

It was over an hour later before their paths crossed again. Miranda was going through her paperwork when she heard a rap on her open door. She looked up to see Jack in the doorway, holding two mugs of coffee. 'Peace offering,' he said.

She smiled ruefully. 'I was out of order. I should be the one apologising—you were trying to be nice.'

'And you just wanted to be left alone. I should have respected your space.' He put one of the mugs down on her desk and sat down.

She took a swig of coffee. 'Thanks for that. So, what can I do for you?'

'New admission,' he said. 'Stella Flowers. She's had anginal chest pain but her angiogram was normal. I've gone through her notes and her GP's already checked that she doesn't have any kind of oesophageal condition or muscular-skeletal pain.'

Miranda thought about it. 'Could be microvascular angina. What about her oestrogen levels?'

Low oestrogen could also affect the linings of the smaller blood vessels. 'I'll order blood tests.'

'What about a thallium scan?' A thallium scan could show narrowing of the smaller arteries, which an angiogram didn't pick up.

'I'll get onto it. I was wondering about cardiac syndrome X. She's post-menopausal and she's got at least three of the six signs. She's got high blood pressure and her blood tests show her HDL levels are down and her triglycerides are up.' HDL or high-density lipoprotein was 'good' cholesterol, which carried excess cholesterol back to the liver. Triglycerides were the main type of fat found in adipose tissue and contributed to arteries furring up.

'Any sign of glucose intolerance or insulin resistance?'

'Her blood-sugar levels were up. So what do you think?'

Miranda sighed. 'Don't tell me. She's overweight, doesn't have time to exercise and anything she puts in her mouth is likely to be high in sugar or refined carbohydrates.'

'Got it in one.'

'It's sounding more and more like cardiac syndrome X,' Miranda said. 'But I suppose there's some good news. If it's that, she's less likely to develop a heart attack than if the pain's caused by narrowed arteries.'

'So it's the usual spiel about diet, exercise and watch your stress levels?'

'Yep. But do the thallium scan, just to be on the safe side.' She gave him a sidelong glance. 'You didn't need my advice at all, did you?'

'In a word—no.'

When had he developed that mischievous-little-boy smile? Hell. Dark and brooding and intense she could handle. She could ignore him in sex-god mode. *This* got completely under her skin. 'So why did you want to see me?'

'Because.'

She glowered, guessing what he hadn't said. He knew how upset she was about the watch—and he'd wanted to check that she was OK. 'Stop fussing. I'm perfectly all right.'

'Sure you are.'

'Jack, get off my case.'

'Friends look out for each other,' he said softly.

Were they friends? No. She didn't want to examine her

feelings about Jack Sawyer right now. They were too complicated.

'Hey.' He leaned over and brushed her cheek with the backs of his fingers, and she felt as if she'd been scorched. 'I'm here if you want to talk. OK?'

'Thanks, but I'm fine.' This wasn't fair. How come he could just cut through her usual barriers? Or undermine them. Whatever. It was just…unsettling.

'You know where I am if you want me.'

It was an offer any female with blood in her veins would simply have jumped at. But she couldn't do it. He didn't mean it like that anyway—did he? 'Cheers,' she muttered, relieved when he left her office.

Miranda was just about to go off duty when her phone rang. 'Hi, it's Kev from the medical assessment unit,' the voice in her ear told her. 'We've got a patient with what we think is viral pericarditis—but we need a cardiologist's view.'

In other words, hers. 'Sure.' If it was pericarditis, the patient would need a bed on her unit. She glanced out of her office window, where she could see the ward's whiteboard. 'You're in luck—if we need it, there's a bed free. I'm on my way now.'

'Off home?' Jack asked as she met him in the corridor.

'No—Kev from the MAU wants me to have a look at a patient.'

'I'll do it, if you like.'

'If you've got a few minutes, I think they could do with both of us. They think the patient has pericarditis.'

This meant that the membranes enveloping the heart were inflamed and filled with fluid. If it was left, the pressure between the membranes rose so the heart couldn't fill properly and stopped pumping—an emergency situation known as cardiac tamponade.

If it wasn't pericarditis, it could be heart failure. But they needed to make sure the diagnosis was correct because the drugs that helped heart failure could cause someone with pericarditis to collapse.

'Let's go,' Jack said.

Kev met them at the door to MAU. 'His name's Liam Redding. He's twenty-eight, a primary school teacher. He was off sick with a virus a few weeks back and thought he was over it—but he's had chest pain for a couple of days, a hacking cough and a fever.'

'Have you done an ECG or an echo?' she asked.

'ECG,' Kev said, passing her a strip.

'ST elevation and an upright T wave,' she said.

Jack read it over her shoulder and nodded. 'We need an echo, just to check there's fluid there,' he said.

Kev took them over to Liam and introduced them.

'Hi, Liam. I'd just like to examine you, if I may?' Miranda asked.

Liam nodded, and winced.

'It hurts when you move?' Miranda guessed.

'Yes,' Liam whispered.

'What about when you swallow?'

'Yes.'

'Try leaning forward a little,' Miranda suggested.

'It's a bit better,' Liam said.

'OK.' Miranda placed her hand gently on Liam's breastbone and pressed lightly.

'That's bad,' he whispered.

'Sorry, sweetheart. I won't do it again. I'm going to listen to your chest and give you an echocardiogram, which won't hurt—but I'm fairly sure that you've got viral pericarditis. Kev tells me you were ill recently.'

'Everyone in the school had it,' he said.

'Probably the Coxsackie B virus—it's one of the most common viruses causing pericarditis,' Miranda said. 'There's a bag of membranes around your heart—the outer layer is tough and the inner layer a sheet attaching to the outer layer and a sheet attaching to the heart. There's a little bit of fluid between them, and when you've got pericarditis the membranes are inflamed. That compresses your heart and stops it working properly— that's why it's been hurting.'

'So I'm not having a heart attack?'

'No,' Jack said. 'You'll find the pain's better when you're sitting down and leaning forward, but it's worse when you're standing or lying down,' he added. 'We need to keep an eye on you in hospital for a few days, to make sure the fluid goes back to normal levels, but the good news is that most people recover without any problems. We can do something about the pain and the cough, too.'

'Thanks,' Liam whispered.

Miranda listened to Liam's heart. As she'd suspected, when she placed the stethoscope on the left edge of Liam's breastbone, she heard a pericardial rub—a sound like hair being rubbed between her fingers. Though, as it could often be mistaken for the sound of the stethoscope moving against the patient's skin, she asked Jack for a second opinion.

'Definite rub,' he agreed.

They transferred Liam to the ward and Jack set up the echo. 'What we're going to do is put a sound recorder on your chest to show us what your heart muscle's doing. We'll put some jelly on your chest to help the probe pick up the sounds, and it'll give us an image of your heart.

It'll take a bit of time, but it won't hurt. If you start feeling worse, just tell us and we'll stop.'

'OK,' Liam said, his voice hoarse.

The echocardiogram showed fluid around the outside of the heart.

'We'll need to keep a close eye on him,' she said quietly to Jack.

'Are you thinking potential tamponade?' he asked, equally quietly, so that Liam couldn't pick up what they were saying and start worrying.

'Or heart failure.' She raised her voice slightly. 'Is there anyone you'd like us to call, Liam?'

'My girlfriend.' He closed his eyes. 'No. Better not. She's away on a course.'

'I'm sure she'd want to know,' Miranda said.

He shook his head. 'Her career comes first.'

Miranda could understand that. Hadn't that been what she'd promised herself for years? And it was one of the reasons she'd made consultant at thirty-two. 'We can tell her that she doesn't have to rush back—you should make a full recovery.'

'The fluid usually disappears of its own accord,' Jack said. 'It'll take somewhere between one and three weeks to do it, so we'll keep you in on bed rest for observation for few days. We'll also give you some anti-inflammatories to help with the pain and make the fluid absorb more quickly—you'll need to keep taking them for a couple of months.'

'You might also get some chest pains over the next few months, so I'd advise against any really vigorous exercise until you've recovered,' Miranda added.

'I'm in training for the marathon,' Liam said. 'With Sarah—my girlfriend.'

'Sorry—you'll have to cheer her on from the sidelines this year,' Miranda told him. 'But walking's good.'

'We're going to take you up to the ward now,' Jack said. 'We'll settle you in and get one of the nurses to monitor you—if the fluid starts building up, we'll need to draw some of it off to make you more comfortable.'

Liam nodded weakly.

On their way back to the unit Jack reminded Miranda that she was supposed to be off duty.

'I'd rather stay for a bit,' she said.

He frowned. 'I can cope, you know.'

'I know. It's not that.'

'What, then?'

'I've got one of my feelings,' she said. 'I just want to stick around. Maybe make those changes to the proposal that you suggested.' She smiled. 'That makes you co-author, if you're OK with that.'

'You did all the work.'

'No. I did the first draft,' she corrected. 'You did the rest.'

'Thanks.'

Miranda was working on the paper when Hannah burst into her office. 'Miranda, Jack asked me to get you.'

'Liam?'

'Yes.'

So her instincts had been right. 'I'm coming now.' She pressed the button to save her file, then walked quickly to Liam's room.

'I need a second opinion on this one,' Jack said quietly. 'He's tachycardic and his JVP's up.' A fast heartbeat and an elevated jugular venous pulse often signalled heart failure—but they could also be symptoms of cardiac tamponade.

'What's his blood pressure?'

'Ninety-five over 65.' Jack glanced at the monitor. 'And dropping.'

Rising JVP and falling blood pressure. If his heart sounds were muffled, too, that would be the classic Beck's triad, which would make it more likely that Liam had cardiac tamponade. She listened to his chest and sighed inwardly as she realised that the heartbeat was muffled. Liam's hand felt cool and clammy, and when she took his pulse she noted that it faded when he breathed in—a condition known as pulsus paradoxus.

'It's tamponade,' she confirmed. 'Have you done a peri-cardiocentesis before?'

'One,' Jack admitted.

'OK. Liam, I'm going to put a needle into your chest to take some of the fluid from around your heart and make you more comfortable,' she said gently. 'Jack, can you give him a local anaesthetic and sedate him?'

Jack nodded and took the syringe.

'Hannah, these are quite rare,' she said to the student. 'It can be hard to tell the difference between heart failure and tamponade.'

'So always get a senior to check?' Hannah asked.

'Yep. I need a twenty-mil syringe, a long eighteen-gauge cannula, a three-way tap and some skin cleanser. Can you get them for me, please, while I put Liam into the right position?'

'Sure.' Hannah went to fetch the equipment while Miranda placed Liam in a half-sitting position.

'What do you know about the xiphoid process?' Jack asked when Hannah handed the syringe to Miranda.

'It's the leaf-shaped projection at the bottom of the breastbone,' Hannah recited.

'Good. What I'm going to do is put the needle in just

underneath it,' Miranda said as she cleaned the injection site on Liam's skin, 'and angle it up and towards his left shoulder. Sometimes you feel a pop as the needle goes into the pericardium. As you go forward with the needle, you try to withdraw the fluid.' Her actions followed her words. 'Keep an eye on the ECG,' she said to Hannah. 'If the ST segment goes down, tell me because I'll need to bring the needle back a bit.'

'If you can draw off around twenty millilitres of fluid, it should stop the tamponade,' Jack said.

'It looks like blood,' Hannah said as the fluid trickled slowly into the syringe.

'Exactly. So you need to check it's fluid and not pure blood,' Miranda said. 'That's why I'm using a three-way tap, so I can check.'

Jack handed her a paper towel, and Miranda smiled. She hadn't even needed to ask him. 'If you put a couple of drops of the fluid on a paper towel,' she explained to Hannah, 'you can see whether it's pure blood or bloody fluid. If it clots, it's blood and you've entered the ventricle.' She performed the test—to her relief, there was no clotting. 'Excellent. It's just fluid,' she said. 'Just what we wanted. OK, Liam, I'm going to take a bit more off now to make you comfortable.' She withdrew as much of the fluid as she could. 'I think it's viral, but I'm going to leave a drain in until we know it's definitely viral and not bacterial. Hannah, I need this sample taken down to the lab, please—I want them to do a culture on the fluid. Better check for TB while they're at it.'

Hannah nodded. 'I'm on my way now.'

'I'm staying for a bit,' she told Jack when they'd settled Liam and made him comfortable again.

'One of your feelings?'

'I don't think so, but you know as well as I do that

there can be complications. I didn't hit the ventricle and I'm pretty sure I didn't touch any of the arteries or puncture the aorta, oesophagus or peritoneum—' she named some of the nastier complications following a pericardiocentesis '—but he might go into VF. Or he might need more fluid drained off.'

Jack nodded. 'Go and get a sandwich or something. I'll bleep you if we hit problems.'

'Thanks, but I'm not hungry.'

Two hours later, when they'd had to draw off more fluid and shock Liam out of VF, Jack said ruefully, 'I hope you don't get any more of your "feelings". They're trouble.'

'Yeah. Look, you're supposed to be off duty now.'

'So are you.'

'I'm pulling rank. Go home.'

'I'm not listening. Want a coffee?'

She shook her head. 'Any more caffeine today, and I'll be flying.'

When they were sure that Liam had stabilised, Jack looked at Miranda. 'Home. You're on early tomorrow.'

'So are you,' she pointed out.

'They'll bleep us if we're needed—and I can be here in less than ten minutes. I live just round the corner.'

So did she. 'OK.'

As they reached the hospital entrance, Jack nudged her. 'I'm starving. Fancy a toasted cheese sandwich?'

'The canteen won't be open.'

'I'll make us one. Though, um, I'll have to get supplies in. Detour to the supermarket?'

She should have just said no. But she was too tired to think straight. 'I've got supplies. Let's go back to my place.'

'If you're sure?'

No, she wasn't sure. She didn't usually let people into her personal space. But she was tired—and, even though Liam had a good chance of survival, Imogen Parker was still fresh in her mind. Right now she didn't want to be on her own. And if that meant letting Jack a little closer…so be it.

They walked in silence to her road—but it was a comfortable silence. Jack Sawyer was easy to be with, she thought. Maybe too easy for her peace of mind.

'I'm on the top floor. Sorry, there isn't a lift,' Miranda said as she unlocked her front door.

CHAPTER SIX

AND he'd thought she was a bit out of his league. He hadn't even been close! Miranda lived in one of the new apartments overlooking the river, and even a one-bedroom flat in this development cost four times his salary—and then some. This wasn't a world he was used to. There were fresh flowers on polished tables in the stairwells, the carpet was immaculate, the stairs were well lit and there were tasteful framed prints on the walls. And that was just in the *shared* area.

Part of Jack wanted to see her to her door, then make some excuse and leave. But a larger part of him was curious. He wanted to see where she lived, what the place was like inside. Whether it would be the same kind of strange mixture as Miranda herself—the cool and efficient doctor who was a party animal and had her navel pierced, the woman who exuded sex but made it clear her career came before everything else. Her desk at work was always clear—did that mean she was messy at home?

'Take a seat,' she said, ushering him inside. 'I'll make us a sandwich—or would you like cheese on toast?'

'I'll do it. Point me to the kitchen and put your feet up.'

'Jack—'

'Or are you one of these women who's possessive about her kitchen?'

She smiled wryly. 'OK. You win. I'll make us a drink and you do the sandwich.'

Her living room was amazing—a light and airy room that stretched the width of the flat. It overlooked the street at one end and there were French doors at the other end, which he imagined led onto a terrace overlooking the river. The walls were painted old gold, the floor was solid polished wood rather than laminate, with some silk kelims scattered on it to break up the expanse of wood, and the curtains were cream and floor-length. There were framed pictures on the wall, including a huge reproduction of some white lilies, the low bookcase was stuffed with medical textbooks and some well-worn paperbacks, in what looked like alphabetical order, and there were three floor-to-ceiling towers housing CDs. He'd never seen so much music outside a CD shop. There was no TV, he noticed, but her sound system was a micro system from a top-quality manufacturer—the type he'd lusted after for years, but he'd never been able to justify the expense to himself.

'The kitchen's through here.' It, too, was stylish and impeccably neat. The units were Shaker-style, in beech, with etched glass doors in the top cabinets and granite work surfaces. There was nothing on the work surfaces apart from a beech breadbin and a block of Japanese knives, plus a vase of irises on the window-sill. All the appliances were hidden away behind beech doors. To Jack, it looked more like a show kitchen than a home. But…hadn't she said she enjoyed cooking? It didn't add up.

'Fridge, oven, bread.' She pointed them out to him, then paused. 'If I drink coffee this late, I'll never get to sleep. But would you like one?'

'I'll have whatever you're having.'

'Hot milk.'

'Perfect. Hot milk and cheese on toast—the ultimate

comfort food.' He set to work—a quick check in her extremely tidy cupboards revealed a bottle of Worcestershire sauce, to his delight—and the cheese on toast was ready at the same time as the milk.

He joined her at the little table at the far end of the kitchen. 'Mmm. Gorgeous. Where do you buy your bread?' he asked after the first bite.

'I don't. I make it myself.'

He raised an eyebrow. So she hadn't been teasing Sid Patterson earlier. 'Is there anything you're not good at?'

She gave him a rueful smile. 'Parking, for starters.'

He grinned back. 'How could I forget?' Then he looked into her eyes. His smile faded and all his good intentions of being 'just friends' crumbled into dust. 'Miranda, are you seeing anyone at the moment?'

'No.'

So far, so good. 'Then would you…?' He took a deep breath. 'Look, I know it could be awkward, with us working together, but I'd like to get to know you better. A lot better.'

She shook her heard. 'I don't do relationships.'

'Neither do I,' he said softly. 'But there's something about you. Something that makes me want to try.'

'I wouldn't be good for you, Jack.'

'Because you're the clinical director's daughter?' He spread his hands. 'I couldn't care less who your father is. I'm not asking him out—I'm asking *you* out.'

'Thank you. I'm flattered. But I can't.'

He needed to know. 'Because of Jordan Francis?'

'No. There isn't anyone in my life. And that's the way I want it.'

Why would a woman as beautiful, talented and down-right nice as Miranda want to stay on her own for the rest of her life? He had a feeling that someone had hurt her badly. *Really* badly. And it made him want to hold her close, soothe her fears away, teach her to trust again. 'Miranda—'

'I don't want to discuss it.' She stared at her half-eaten sandwich. 'I'm tired, Jack. I'd prefer you to go now, please.'

'OK. I won't push you.' If he did, he knew she'd never give him another chance.

'Thank you. I'll see you tomorrow.'

He glanced at his watch. 'Today, actually. Thanks for supper.'

'Pleasure.' Her voice was cool and polite. It was clear she really, really wanted him to go. Though he really, really wanted to stay. Unable to resist touching her, he stroked her cheek with the backs of his fingers. 'Sleep well. I'll see myself out.'

Sleep well? That was a joke, Miranda thought an hour later when she turned over in bed and pummelled her pillow yet again. Why, why, why had he touched her like that? A gentle little gesture, telling her without words that he understood and wasn't going to push her. That she could trust him.

I'd like to get to know you better… There's something about you… His words echoed in her mind.

He'd been right about one thing. It *would* be awkward at work if they got together. It would be much more sensible to keep their relationship strictly business. She'd just have to try harder, that was all.

When her alarm beeped at six, she had to drag herself out of bed. It took a cold shower and two cups of double-strength coffee before her head decided it wasn't stuffed with cotton wool after all. By the time she'd walked to work, she'd managed to find her usual cool detachment.

Her shift crossed only partially with Jack's and she kept the conversation strictly to work-related matters.

His eyes said what she wouldn't let his mouth say, though, and she had another sleepless night. Friday and Saturday were more of the same, but at least she had Sunday off. An hour at her dance class worked most of her demons off, and she was about to go home and attack her ironing pile with renewed vigour when a voice drawled behind her, 'We really must stop meeting like this, Miss Turner.'

Calderford wasn't that huge a place, and Jack had told her he lived near the hospital. Of course they were bound to run into each other. 'Yes. People might talk,' she said coolly, trying to match his tone.

And then she made the mistake of looking at him.

On the dance-floor he'd looked good. In a pair of black cargo pants, a black cotton sweater, black running shoes, a pair of sunglasses and a slight touch of stubble he looked incredible. Like a film star. And he was wearing that little-boy grin again. Completely irresistible. Hell and double hell. She had to keep this light, cool and professional—before her libido took over and she leapt on him.

'So what have you been up to?' she asked. Stupid question. Dressed like that and carrying a gym bag, there was only one thing he could have been doing! She hastily suppressed the vision of Jack in a T-shirt and shorts.

He nodded towards the building she'd just left. 'Working out.' He glanced at her bag. 'I didn't see you in there.'

'I wasn't. There's a studio above the gym,' she explained. 'I went to a dance class.'

'Zydeco?' he guessed.

'Egyptian.'

Oh, no. The vision that raised was way too much for his self control. Miranda in harem pants and a skimpy top, barefoot and shimmying so the diamond in her navel caught the light… His mouth dried. 'Belly-dancing?' he mumbled.

'In a floor-length dress,' she said. 'Forget the seven veils bit.'

How could he? Especially as she was the one who'd brought it up! His mouth stopped working in synch with his brain—this was, after all, the woman who'd spent the last three days freezing him out at work, barely saying a single syllable that didn't involve a patient's case history. She'd told him to back off. So why on earth was he saying this? 'It's nearly lunchtime. Come and have lunch with me?'

'Where?'

Where? At least it wasn't an outright no. Although bits of him wanted to sweep her off her feet and carry her back to his little terraced house, he knew that would be a bad move. For his own sanity, among other things. 'There's a wine bar round the corner. They do reasonable food,' he said.

'OK. Provided we go Dutch.'

'Fine.' She was going to have lunch with him. She was actually going to have lunch with him outside the hospital. He felt like a teenager on his first date, all sweaty palms and erratic heartbeat. Right at that moment he wouldn't have been surprised to find his face was covered in pimples and bits of wispy hair—or that his voice had suddenly gone up an octave.

They found a quiet table in a corner of the wine bar. Jack watched Miranda as she studied the menu. Her hair was pulled back, but not as severely as she wore it at work.

He resisted the temptation to reach over and remove the scrunchie. Just.

'What do you recommend?' she asked finally.

'The pasta's good.'

'Then I'll have the fettucini Alfredo, please, with a green salad.'

'What would you like to drink?'

'Dry white wine, please,' she said. When he returned to their table, she nodded at his orange juice. 'Are you on duty or driving somewhere this afternoon?'

'No.'

'So you're teetotal?'

He nodded. He didn't drink. *Ever.*

'Do you mind me drinking wine, then?'

'No, it's fine.'

He could sense her staring at him. And then he heard the question he dreaded. 'Why don't you drink?'

'I just don't.'

'Sorry. I didn't, um, mean to pry.'

He looked at her, noting the bright pink spots in the middle of her cheeks. 'Sorry. I didn't mean to snap. It's just...' Well, why shouldn't he tell her? She'd understand. From what he'd seen, her relationship with her own father was stormy enough. 'My father was an alcoholic.'

'No wonder you don't want to touch the stuff.'

Not sneering, not patronising. Just plain and simple understanding, he thought in amazement. He'd always thought that if anyone knew about it, from med school onwards, they'd start wondering if he'd go the same way.

'Don't worry, I won't spread it round the hospital.'

Was the panic on his face that obvious? 'I didn't think you would.'

'I'm sorry I pushed you over the orange juice at Louie's.'

He shrugged. 'You weren't to know.'

'It must be hard, helping a recovering alcoholic,' she said.

'I wouldn't know.' His mouth twisted. 'He died when I was fourteen.'

'I'm sorry.' She took his hand and squeezed it.

Having her hold his hand like that was…weird. Comforting. Something in her eyes made him decide to trust her. 'I wish I'd known him when he wasn't a drunk,' Jack said. 'Mum tried to keep it from me and my brothers when we were little, but I was the oldest and I started to notice the smell of drink, the way he always felt rough in the mornings, the fact he never came home until well after we were in bed…' He sighed. 'Whenever we had any money, Dad just drank it away. Mum tried and tried to get him to give up, to see the doctor, to go to a support group—but he refused to admit he had a problem. One day he started throwing up blood.'

'Oesophageal varices?' she guessed.

He nodded. Varicose veins inside the throat were a common problem with alcoholics. 'They managed to stop it but he had a re-bleed. Before they could put a Sengstaken-Blakemore tube in to stop the bleeding and get him to Theatre, he arrested and died.'

'And that's why you decided to become a cardiac specialist?'

'I'd always been interested in how hearts worked.' He gave a rueful smile. 'Though I nearly didn't become a doctor.'

'Why?'

'Dad left us in a lot of debt. Mum only found out about it after he died. He'd kept it all from her. Credit cards, loan sharks—you name it, he'd done it. We had no idea what he'd even spent it all on. I dunno. The horses, maybe. Anyway, I didn't think it was fair to be a student for years when my wages could help the family get back on its feet—but Mum had other ideas. She wouldn't let me give up my dreams.' He bit his lip. 'She used to work in an office during the day and fitted in a few cleaning jobs at night and weekends. My brothers and I mucked in with the chores, and I did the cooking. Then, when I was old enough, I got a job stacking shelves at weekends. We muddled through, and she'd paid off the debts by the time I did my A levels. I was going to get a job, but my brothers filled in the application for med school for me and sent it off.'

'Are they doctors, too?'

He shook his head. 'Charlie's a policeman and Brian became a fitter for a window company. He set up on his own three years back. They've got their own families now, but they live just round the corner from Mum.'

'You're close, then.'

'Yeah.' He smiled. As kids, his brothers had teased him for always having his nose in a book, but he knew they were proud of him. And he'd never forgotten his roots—they all knew that if any of them was in trouble, all they had to do was pick up the phone and he'd be right by their side. He saw them every Sunday afternoon when he wasn't on duty, playing football with the kids and listening to them read, and then they all piled over to his mother's for sandwiches and cake. On impulse, he began, 'Do you want—?'

But before he could ask her to go with him, their pasta arrived. He moved his hand from hers.

'This is good. Very good,' she said after the first mouthful. 'Sorry, you were saying something?'

'Doesn't matter.' On second thoughts, maybe it wouldn't be a good idea to let her meet his family. They were a world away from her own, and he didn't want his mother trying to matchmake and being let down again. Where Miranda Turner was concerned, he wouldn't be the kind of man she'd want to marry, even when he made it to consultant level.

They were worlds apart, Miranda thought. He'd had to struggle to get to med school—the only obstacle she'd had was her father. And even he hadn't been that much of a problem, thanks to May.

Though they did have one thing in common. Jack had obviously found it as hard to get close to his father as she did to hers. 'Did you go to med school here?' she asked.

He nodded. 'Mum wanted me to go to London, but I wanted to stay near—at least I could help out a bit.'

'So you had a job as well as being a student?'

He shrugged. 'Worked as a barman.'

Given his father's alcoholism, that must have hurt. But having a close family…she envied him that. Miranda wasn't even close to her mother. As far back as she could remember her mother had been busy with charity work, chairing committees and discussing important issues.

'At least you had your family behind you,' she said softly. The closest family she'd had had been May. And even she had been a two-hour drive away while Miranda had been growing up.

'Didn't your mum want you to be a doctor either?'

She stared at him in shock. How come he knew about her father…? But, then, she'd already told him why she'd trained in Glasgow. When she'd told him about May. And he'd trusted her with his own secrets. It was only fair to tell him hers. 'My mother always followed my father's lead.'

'I'm sorry.'

Miranda shrugged. 'I learned to live with it.'

'If you'd applied to study at Calderford, wouldn't he have come to terms with it?'

'I don't know. But I didn't want to risk it.' She sighed. 'I don't even know what he wanted me to do. Be like my mother, I suppose—settle down and get married, probably to a banker who'd give me a house in the country, four children and a dog. Oh, and do charity work.'

'Would that have been so bad?'

Maybe. Maybe not. But what had happened with Rupert had been much, much worse. Not that she could tell Jack about that. Even the thought of it made her want to crawl into a dark cave somewhere and howl. 'I wanted to be a doctor. Same as you.'

'So you went to Glasgow.'

She nodded. 'My father wasn't very happy about it, but May was supporting me so he couldn't do anything. I don't think he ever forgave her—which made me feel even worse when she died. Maybe if she'd been on good terms with him, she wouldn't have—'

'Hey.' He reached out and squeezed her hand. 'It doesn't work like that. Even if they'd been the best of friends, she might have had a heart attack when she was out somewhere.'

'I suppose.'

'Did he come to your graduation?'

She shook her head. 'He had an important meeting. May came.'

'What about your mum?'

'There was a charity do. As the chair of the committee, she had to be there.' She smiled wearily. 'I suppose that's one of the reasons why I applied for the job here. If I was right under his nose, he'd have to accept my choice of career.'

'And respect the fact you were good enough to be a consultant.'

She shrugged. 'Maybe I just need a sex change.'

He blinked. 'How come? The Prof isn't sexist.'

'Maybe not at work. But I'm his daughter.' She frowned. 'I think he always wanted a son to follow in his footsteps and become a paediatrician. Except my mother couldn't have any more children, so he was stuck with me.'

'You could always switch to paediatrics. Specialise in paediatric cardiology.'

'But I still wouldn't be his boy.' She sighed. 'That's the worst bit of being an only child. Your parents pin all their hopes on you, and if you disappoint them…'

'I guess.' Jack raised his glass. 'Let's have a toast. To difficult parents.'

'Difficult parents.'

'I got through it,' he said softly. 'And so will you.'

To have someone else believe in her—after all these years—was almost her undoing. She finished her meal in silence.

'Pudding?' he asked.

Miranda shook her head. 'Not for me, thanks.'

'Coffee?'

'No, thanks. Anyway, I'd better let you get on.'

He glanced at his watch. 'Yes—I should have been at Mum's half an hour ago.'

'Sorry.'

'No problem.' He signalled a waiter for the bill, and Miranda insisted on splitting it equally.

'Thanks for lunch,' she said. 'I enjoyed it.'

'Me, too.' He paused. 'Tomorrow…you're off too, aren't you?'

'Ye-es.'

'Come and make sandcastles with me. As mates. Pick you up at ten?'

No. She was supposed to say no. But her mouth was working to a different agenda. 'All right. See you at ten.'

CHAPTER SEVEN

MIRANDA couldn't remember the last time she'd been to the seaside. Or built sandcastles. Jack beat her hands down, so she had to buy the ice creams. And then he insisted on going for a paddle in the North Sea.

'At the beginning of April? You're crazy,' she said, giggling.

'Come on. It's not going to be that cold.' He gave her a sidelong look, removed his shoes and socks and started rolling up his jeans. 'I dare you. Double-dare you.'

'Right.' She took off her shoes, rolled up her jeans and marched into the waves—and then shrieked at the cold as the water splashed onto her skin. When Jack laughed, she pulled him in next to her and chuckled when he gave a sharp intake of breath. 'Not going to be that cold, you said?'

'So I was wrong.' He gave her a wide smile. 'I'm not perfect.'

Wasn't he? From where she was standing, she wasn't so sure. And that worried her. She couldn't let herself get close to Jack Sawyer. She really couldn't risk it.

But somehow, as they walked along the sand barefoot together, his arm ended up round her shoulders and hers ended up round his waist. And when they reached the cliffs, he spun her round to face him. 'I know we're supposed to be doing this as mates, but...' He lowered his head so that his lips just brushed hers, then pulled back slightly to look into her eyes. 'I want to kiss you. Now.'

His eyes were huge and dark and intense. She'd

thought she could resist him in sex-god mode. How wrong she'd been. Because instead of pulling away and telling him to be sensible, she tipped her head back and offered him her mouth. And he kissed her. Kissed her until she was dizzy and had to cling to him. Kissed her until her toes were tingling. Kissed her until she wished they were somewhere a lot more private. Kissed her until a couple of passing teenagers wolf-whistled them and broke the spell.

They drew apart and just stared at each other.

'That wasn't supposed to happen,' she said.

'I know.' He looked as dazed as she felt.

'We're colleagues.'

'You're my boss,' he corrected.

She wrinkled her nose. 'I don't care.'

He gave her a slow, sweet smile that made her heart flutter. 'Neither do I.'

'Jack—'

'Shh.' He laid the tip of one finger on her lips. 'Not now. Let's just *be*.'

She nodded, and they walked on together, arms wrapped round each other. Crazy. If she thought about it, this was the most stupid thing she could possibly do. If the hospital grapevine heard even a whisper of this...

But it felt good to be in his arms. Safe and warm and wanted.

When they'd walked back to the car, Jack drove them to a small seaside fish and chip shop. 'Best fish and chips in Tyneside,' he told her. 'And they have to be eaten straight from the paper.'

He was right. The chips were perfect, crisp on the outside and soft on the inside, seasoned liberally with salt and vinegar, and the batter on the fish melted in her mouth. Miranda couldn't remember the last time she'd enjoyed herself this much.

And then, all too soon, they were back on the outskirts of Calderford. 'Coffee at my place?' he asked.

She nodded, curious to see what his home was like.

The small terraced house was everything she'd half expected. Tidy and clean, very simply furnished. But there were children's pictures stuck to his fridge with magnets, all labelled 'To Uncle Jack' with lots of kisses beneath the signatures. There were framed photographs all along the mantelpiece in his living room—Jack, wearing his graduation robes, with his arm round a woman who looked so much like him she had to be his mother. Another of Jack and two men—clearly his brothers— grinning broadly, their arms round each other. Wedding and christening pictures, too—Jack had obviously been best man to both his brothers, and godfather to his nieces and nephews. This was definitely the home of a family man.

So how come he wasn't married? Or had he been married, but was now divorced? Or had it just been that, like her, he'd been driven to concentrate on his career and just hadn't had time for a relationship?

'One black coffee.'

'Thanks.' She cupped her hands round the mug and stared into the dark liquid.

He sighed. 'You can relax. I'm not going to throw you over my shoulder and haul you upstairs to my bed.'

Her skin heated as her gaze met his. 'I didn't think you were.' No, that was a lie. She *had* thought about it. Was thinking about it even more now he'd said it.

'Hey. I said I wanted to get to know you better.' He moistened his lower lip with his tongue and her pulse rate speeded up another notch. 'Yes, of course I want to go to bed with you. You're gorgeous and I don't think any man could resist you. And, actually, I'd quite like to do the caveman thing.' He gave her a rueful grin. 'But it wouldn't be fair to either of us.'

So what was he saying? That what was happening between them had to stop?

Jack placed his mug on the mantelpiece, did the same with hers and lifted her hands to his lips. 'My self-control isn't that brilliant. I wasn't planning to seduce you, so I'm not…prepared. I don't keep a pack of condoms just on the off-chance—I've never been like that. I'm Jack, yes, but not ''Jack the lad''.'

Miranda's flush deepened. His self-control was a damned sight better than hers. Contraception had been the last thing on her mind.

He kissed each finger in turn. 'So. What are we going to do about it?'

'I don't know.'

'You don't do relationships. Neither do I. You're my boss and it'd make life complicated. And you're out of my league. I know all that. But it doesn't stop me wanting you. Since you walked onto my ward, I've gone…' He paused, searching for the right word. 'Haywire.'

Her throat was so dry she could hardly get the words out. 'Me, too. And I'm not.'

'What?'

'Out of your league.'

He raised an eyebrow. 'Oh, come on. You're the Professor's daughter.'

'It's not important.'

'Isn't it?'

The chip on his shoulder wasn't that deep. This was his way of giving her a get-out, she knew. Meaning that she could stop this any time she wanted. And yet…she didn't want to stop. 'No. It's really *not* important,' she said softly. She stood on tiptoe and kissed him lightly on the lips.

'So are you saying you want to give us a try?'

Yes. But…she couldn't forget the past. She was pretty sure that Jack wasn't like Rupert—but the only way to make sure her worst nightmare never happened again was to keep their relationship secret. 'As long as it's just between you and me.'

He frowned. 'I'm not with you.'

'We work together. Our relationship—' there, she'd said it '—could cause problems at the hospital.'

Jack stared at her. Hell. It was Jessica all over again. *He's from the wrong side of town—fun for now, but he's not the kind of man you'd marry.* Miranda wanted to be with him, but she was ashamed of him. After all, what was he? The son of a drunk. A man who lived in a tiny little terrace instead of a huge country mansion or a flat on a stylish development. Not that he was going to tell her why he lived here. It was none of her business that he was buying his mother's house for her.

It was never going to work.

He lifted his chin. 'In that case, perhaps we'd better fo—'

'It's not you, it's me. I'm not good at relationships, Jack,' she cut in. 'If you want the truth, I'm lousy at them.'

Well, that would explain why she never dated the same man more than twice.

Her mouth twisted. 'Like you, I feel I've gone haywire since I met you. I'm not used to that feeling—of not being in control of myself. The idea of seeing you…being your girlfriend, lover, whatever…it's like stepping off the edge of a precipice.'

'And you're scared neither of us has a parachute?'

She nodded.

'That makes two of us.' He smiled wryly. 'So, we have a choice. We can try and pretend this isn't happening and hope it blows over. Or we can step off the precipice together.'

He was still holding her hands. She tightened her fingers round his. 'On the ward, it's going to be the same as it always was between us. Colleagues. And outside...'

'Outside, you're my girl,' he said softly.

'Yes.'

He knew he needed to go gently now. 'Thank you. I'll drive you home. If you change your mind tomorrow, that's fine. I won't push you.'

'And if I don't?'

He lifted her hand to his lips and kissed it. 'Then tomorrow night we get take-away pizza, sit on your balcony and watch the stars.'

Miranda was up early the next morning. She'd slept badly and she couldn't settle to anything at home—she even spilled a box of cereal over her kitchen floor because she couldn't concentrate. She was full of the jitters. Had Jack meant it? Would he really be detached and professional with her at work?

To her relief, he was. He stayed completely out of her way, apart from a brief discussion with her about a patient with Wolff-Parkinson-White syndrome—a condition where there was an extra pathway leading from the upper to the lower part of the heart, which interfered with the heart's pumping action and caused a rapid heartbeat and palpitations.

Jack talked her quickly through the patient's history, then showed her the ECG and echo. 'I think an RF ablation's the best thing here. Unless you found that surgery was better in Glasgow?'

'Catheter ablation's fine,' she said. 'Hannah, this might be interesting for you to see.'

'Definitely,' Jack said. He explained the condition to their student. 'So what we're going to do is called an RF or radio frequency ablation. What that means is we'll pass an electrode through a vein into the heart, with its tip near the extra pathway. We'll apply radio frequencies for between twenty and fifty seconds—that will stop the extra pathway functioning, so the patient won't have the problem any more.'

The young student nodded, her face brightening. Miranda forced herself to ignore a quick stab of jealousy. Hannah might have a crush on Jack—even Claire had remarked on it a couple of days back, saying how Hannah's face lit up whenever Jack walked onto the ward—but nothing was going to happen. Was it?

No, of course not. Not all men were like Rupert. She just had to learn to trust him.

'Doing anything nice tonight?' Leila asked Miranda later in the staff rest room.

Jack went very still. Or maybe she just noticed it because she was watching him. 'A lazy evening—take-away pizza and a bit of stargazing,' she said.

He didn't move. But she could see the relief in his eyes. And the hunger.

At ten o'clock that evening they were curled up together on her balcony with an empty pizza box next to them. Jack's back rested against the French doors and Miranda was leaning back against him, her head resting on his shoulder and his arm wrapped round her waist. 'I love watching the stars. The W-shaped constellation over there's Cassiopeia. That's Orion, the hunter—look, you can see his belt and sword—and there's Sirius, the dog star, by his feet.' Jack pointed out the constellations to her with his free hand. 'There's this amazing cloud of dark gas in the middle of Orion—it's called the Horsehead nebula because it looks like a chess knight. Though you can't see more than a blur of the nebula behind it with the naked eye—even out in the country-side, where you don't have the same amount of light pollution you get in the city. You need a really huge telescope to see properly.'

'How come you know so much about astronomy?' she asked, curious.

'Before my dad…' His voice cracked. 'Well, when I was really small, he used to point them out to me. He even drew me a star map.' He smiled. 'When I was really little, I wanted to be an astronaut. Go to outer space, discover new worlds, walk on the moon… I suppose all kids fantasise like that. My nephew, Rory—that's Brian's eldest—is just as mad on the stars as I was. I took him to the London to see the Planetarium last year. He loved it.'

She could just imagine Jack taking his own children to places like that, talking to them about what they were seeing and letting his own enthusiasm breathe life into it for them. He'd make a great dad, warm and loving and always there for them. Always listening. The kind of dad his father hadn't been.

'Penny for them?' he asked.

She spoke before she thought the consequences through. 'Just thinking what a good dad you'd make.'

He held her closer. 'Maybe. One day.' He rested his cheek against her hair.

Being with him was so, so easy. There was no pressure, no expectations she had to live up to—he just accepted her for what she was. They sat together in a dreamy silence, just watching the stars and enjoying each other's closeness.

Half an hour later he kissed the top of her head. 'I'd better go. I'm on early tomorrow. And I don't want to overstay my welcome.'

Sensible Jack. She appreciated that—but at the same time she also wanted the caveman.

She nearly got the caveman, too, when she twisted round to kiss him. What started off as sweet and gentle quickly turned explosive, and before she knew it she'd half unbuttoned his shirt.

Gently, he took her hands, kissed her fingertips and restored order to his clothes. 'Much as I want to, I don't think it's a good idea. Not on our first date. And, um, perhaps not on your balcony, in full view of anyone who might be walking by the river.' He gave her that mischievous-little-boy grin to take the sting from his words. 'I'd hate you not to respect me in the morning.'

'Ha.' He was right. She knew that. But it didn't stop her wanting him. 'See you tomorrow night?'

'Count on it.' He kissed the tip of her nose. 'Sleep tight.'

The next few days were the happiest Miranda had ever spent. Jack introduced her to his favourite places—the abbey ruins at the far end of town, a Wednesday afternoon walk hand in hand through a wood with a carpet of bluebells, feeding the ducks at the canal, a roller-coaster ride at the funfair further down the coast.

And then he sent her an email. *Pick me up at 7 tonight.*

Where are we going? she sent back.

Exclusive restaurant.

Well, that told her a lot. And also it wasn't his style—
it was almost as if he knew she'd grown up going to
expensive restaurants and fancy places, and he was intro-
ducing her to the simple delights of life. What was he
playing at?

What do I wear? she asked.

It took an age before he responded. *The diamond.*

She grinned. If she turned up to his house wearing
nothing but her navel ring… And then her smile faded,
replaced by a shiver of anticipation. The last few days
had been fantastic. The more she got to know Jack, the
more she liked him. The more she desired him. And he
wanted her to wear the diamond. Her mouth went dry.
Did that mean tonight was *the* night? Tonight was the
night they'd break down the last barriers between them
and make love?

What sort of food? she typed.

*Depends what the chef picks up on his way home to-
night.*

The penny dropped. She smiled. She knew exactly
where the restaurant was. And exactly what she was going to wear.

At seven that evening, Miranda rang Jack's doorbell.

'Hi.'

He looked gorgeous. Dark fitted trousers, a short-
sleeved turquoise silk shirt—and a blue-and-white striped
butcher's apron. It didn't make him look domestic or hen-
pecked. Just very, very sexy. Man the hunter, getting his
woman's work out of the way so she could concentrate
on something more important. Him.

'Hi, yourself.'

She smiled to herself, noting the way he looked
askance at her long coat. Well, she wasn't going to wear

this particular outfit on the street. Even if it *was* only a short distance from her car to his front door.

'Going to take my coat?' she asked, as he closed the front door behind her.

'Of course.' He slid it from her shoulders. Then he looked at her. 'Uh.'

She grinned. 'You told me to wear the diamond.' And she'd remembered the look on his face when he'd bumped into her after her dance class. What better way to show off the navel ring than a pair of black filmy harem pants and a crop top?

'Um…'

A nasty feeling hit her. No. He hadn't intended to introduce her to his family tonight, had he? 'It is just the two of us, isn't it?' she asked, panicking.

He nodded. 'Sorry. I, um…I can't think straight right now. That…' He gestured to the diamond. 'I guess that's a bit more distracting than I bargained for.'

She grinned. 'You asked for it.'

She could have sworn he muttered, 'Oh, yes—please.'

'I brought you these in lieu of wine.'

He accepted the small package with a smile—a smile which broadened to a grin of pure delight as he unwrapped the tissue paper and discovered what it was. Seventy per cent cocoa dark chocolate thins from a very, very exclusive chocolatier. 'Oh, wow. You know my vices. Thanks.' He moved towards her—then took a step back. 'No. If I kiss you now, I'm going to end up not feeding you. And I promised you dinner. Go through to the dining room.'

It was mean. She knew it even as she did it. But she couldn't help teasing him. She kicked off her shoes and did the Egyptian walk, wiggling her bottom and shimmying as she moved. She was rewarded with a low groan, and smiled to herself. Everything was going to be all right.

He'd really made an effort, she realised. A vase of irises on the table and vanilla-scented candles in a pewter candelabrum.

And the meal was spectacular. Prawns with aioli, Spanish chicken served with tiny new potatoes, button mushrooms, green beans and baby corn. And finally the most gorgeous lemon pudding she'd ever tasted, served with fresh raspberries.

'Tell me where you bought it,' she begged.

'I didn't. It's home-made.'

'By you?'

'Don't sound so surprised. I told you, I used to do the cooking. It's my Auntie Michelle's recipe.'

'It's fabulous.'

'Lemon lust tart,' he said.

Lust. Yep, that was a word she knew all about right now. Candlelight suited him—it made him look dark and mysterious. And sexy. *Very* sexy.

'Coffee?' he asked.

'Let me help you.'

He shook his head. 'I'm spoiling you tonight.'

She just stopped herself asking, Is that a promise?

Watching him eat his share of the chocolate thins was torture. His long, well-shaped fingers, his beautiful mouth… She knew how they felt against her skin. But she wanted more. Much more.

This was crazy. Like him, she'd stuck to fizzy mineral water with her meal. And yet she felt as if she'd drunk half a bottle of champagne. Must be his smile that's intoxicating me, she thought.

And then he gave her a lazy, sensual grin that made her heart flip. 'Do me a favour?'

Excitement licked through her veins. What was he going to ask her? 'What?' she asked huskily.

'Dance for me? Please?'

Dance for him. It would be nothing like the dancing she did in her class—the kind of routine she'd work through with a troupe. This would be much more personal. She'd be dancing for her man. She nodded. 'I've got some music in my car.'

'Want me to get it?'

'Please.' She handed him her car keys. He returned a few moments later with three CDs. 'I wasn't sure which one.'

'This one,' she said with a smile, selecting an old favourite. 'Track three.'

'OK.' He ushered her into his living room and slid the CD into his hi-fi, then lit the large church candles which sat at the ends of his mantelpiece and switched off the overhead light. 'Tell me when you're ready.'

'I really need a hip belt to do this justice,' she said. 'The one I use at class has jingles on it. You're supposed to follow the line of my hips,' she informed him. 'But I guess I'll have to improvise.' She reached up and pulled the silk scarf from her hair.

Every nerve-ending in Jack's body went crazy. She must know what effect she was having on him. Dear God, she must know, he thought as she shook her hair so it cascaded onto her shoulders.

She tied the scarf loosely round her hips, then nodded. 'Ready.'

He pressed the 'play' button and slid onto a chair as she began to dance.

She was beautiful. Incredibly beautiful. She swayed in time to the mournful beginning of the music—and then the drums kicked in and her body really moved, weaving sinuously, shimmying until he was dizzy with wanting her. The diamond in her navel glittered in the candlelight and he had a tough time staying put—he wanted to leap up and carry her off to his bed, right there and then.

When the track finished, he couldn't stop himself. He was at her side in a nanosecond, pulled her into his arms and kissed her thoroughly.

'I take it you liked it?' she asked huskily, when he broke the kiss.

'Uh.' He kissed her again. 'You're about the only woman who's ever made me speechless. I had all these good intentions for tonight—and they've all gone to hell in a handcart. I want you, Miranda.' He ran his fingers through her hair, marvelling at its silkiness. 'I want you *now*.'

'How much?' she whispered.

In answer, he pulled her against his body so she could feel his reaction to her. 'This much.'

'Mmm.'

He nuzzled her cheek. 'And?'

'Yes.'

'Forgive me for this,' he said. 'But I really, really can't help myself.' He picked her up, blew out the candles and carried her up the stairs.

He kicked his bedroom door open, then let her slide down his body until her feet touched the floor.

And then, to her shock, he took a step back. No. Please, no. He wasn't going to reject her now, was he?

'Miranda. I want you—I want you more than I've ever wanted anyone in my entire life. But I don't want to push you into something you're not ready for.'

Her heart melted. 'You're giving me a chance to back out?'

'Uh-huh.' His fingers were laced so tightly together his

knuckles were white. This was clearly killing him. But he cared enough to make sure it was what she wanted, too.

She smiled, untied the scarf from her hips and dropped it on the floor. 'Your turn.'

His shirt hit the deck in seconds. 'Yours,' he said huskily.

She removed the crop top to reveal a black lace bra. 'Yours.'

He narrowed his eyes. 'You're wearing more than I am.'

'Your turn,' she repeated.

He grinned, and removed one sock. When she folded her arms, he gave a shrug of defeat and removed the other. 'Yours,' he said softly.

She let the harem pants fall to the floor, revealing knickers to match her bra. 'Yours.'

His trousers hit the floor. And she'd never seen anything as sexy as the black knit jockey shorts he was wearing. They clung to his hard, toned body like a second skin. And she wanted him. She wanted him *now*.

'Your turn,' he whispered.

In response, she crooked her index finger, beckoning him. 'Yours.'

He drew his finger slowly down her breastbone, dipping it into her cleavage. 'Your skin's so soft,' he breathed. 'I want to…' He undid her bra with one hand and bent to nuzzle her breasts.

She gasped, tipping her head back, and he took one nipple into his mouth, teasing the other with his fingers.

'Birthday, Christmas, Valentine's Day…all at once,' he murmured against her skin. He dropped to his knees and drew a circle round her navel with his tongue. 'And now it's time to unwrap my present…' Gently, he eased her knickers down. Touched her. Tasted her.

Miranda pushed her shaking hands into his hair, urging him on. She lost all sense of time, of what was happening—all she could concentrate on was the way Jack made her feel, the glorious sensations surging through her. And the second before she hit the peak, she realised that he was lying naked on the bed, she was astride him—and then he entered her.

She cried out his name, feeling as though she were in the middle of a vortex. And then his hands were gripping hers, holding her up. The first wave passed, and she began to move over him, gaining in confidence.

'You're so beautiful,' he murmured. 'Tell me I'm not dreaming. Tell me you're really here with me.'

She lifted their joined hands to her mouth, and kissed each of his knuckles in turn. 'It's real.'

'Is it? Or are we in paradise somewhere?' He tilted his pelvis slightly, moving with her, and it was her turn to be speechless.

'Uh.'

'Mmm. What happened to my cool, controlled consultant?' he teased.

'You did,' she gasped. 'You did.'

At that, Jack kissed her. Soft and sweet and cherishing—and then it exploded into fire. Miranda felt the pressure rising, rising, rising—as she hit the peak again she cried out, heard his answering cry as his body surged.

Later—she had no idea how much time later—she lay curled in his arms. He was stroking her hair and his other hand rested lightly on her hip.

'I didn't know it could be like that,' he said. 'Miranda. O brave new world that has such a woman in it.'

A deliberate misquote, she knew. 'That's supposed to be my line, isn't it?'

'I always thought Ferdinand was a wimp.' He dropped a kiss on her forehead.

'How come you know Shakespeare?'

He stiffened slightly. 'And why shouldn't I?'

'You're a scientist. Most people do arts or sciences, not both.'

'I did *The Tempest* for my GCSE. And I knocked around with some English students in my first year. My room-mate joined the university players and persuaded me to help him learn his lines.' He held her closer. '"Age cannot wither her, nor custom stale Her infinite variety." Enobarbus, on Cleopatra.' He paused. 'And you'll still be beautiful when we're ninety.'

Had he just said 'you're' or 'we're'? A shiver of pleasure ran through her. 'You're not so bad yourself. Though I don't know as much poetry as you do, so I can't return the compliment.'

'Maybe I can teach you.'

She slid her fingers across his torso. 'Private tuition. Hmm. What are your rates?'

He gasped as her hand slipped lower. 'Mmm. That's a start...'

Later still, Jack kissed the tip of her nose. 'Stay with me tonight?'

Miranda shook her head. 'I didn't bring any spare clothes with me.'

'I've got a brand-new toothbrush,' he offered.

She chuckled. 'Right. And I'm really going to do my rounds in these harem pants tomorrow.'

'Shame. I'd rather like to see that.' He grinned. 'Mind you, it might finish off our patients. The male ones, that is. Better not risk their blood pressure.' He kissed her lightly. 'I'll see you home.'

'I drove here,' she reminded him.

'I'll go with you—I can run back.'

'It's two in the morning.'

'So?'

'So it's not a good time to go for a run.'

'I'd rather you weren't on your own—even if it is a short distance from the road to your front door.'

'I park in a secure compound below the flats,' she said. 'It's safe. Really safe.'

'Are you sure?'

'I'll ring you when I get home to prove it. Even though it'll wake you up.'

'Stay here instead,' he urged. 'Go home in the morning.'

'It's already morning.' She kissed him with regret. 'If I don't go now, I'll never get up in time for my shift. And neither will you.' She sat up.

He took her hand. 'Am I going to see you tonight?'

She nodded. 'My turn to cook for you.'

'Deal.'

'And, Jack?'

'Mmm-hmm?'

'Bring some spare clothes,' she whispered.

CHAPTER EIGHT

LIFE didn't get any better than this, Miranda thought. At work, it was as if she'd always been part of the team, and her father had even agreed to her research proposal. And outside work she had Jack. Jack, who made popcorn for them before they watched an old film at his place. Jack, who tempted her with premium ice cream eaten straight from the tub. Jack, who washed her all over in the bath—and then climbed in with her and made love to her until she was shivering with pleasure and the bath-room floor was flooded and they had to mop it up with spare towels. Jack, who was systematically teaching her the name of every constellation in the sky.

They'd fallen into a routine of spending one night at her place, the next at his. If their duties didn't match, it didn't matter. When she woke in the middle of the night she was lulled back to sleep again by the sound of his heartbeat. And his way of waking her up in the mornings was much, much nicer than her alarm clock: long, slow kisses that quickly heated her blood, followed by love-making that put a smile on her face for the rest of the day.

He kept a razor and a toothbrush in her bathroom cab-inet, and some of her clothes had migrated into his ward-robe. And she was seriously considering giving him her spare key. The only sticking point was Sundays. If he wasn't working, Jack always spent Sundays with his fam-ily. She didn't mind that so much—what she minded was that he hadn't asked her to go with him. But she knew it was her own fault. She was the one who'd insisted on keeping it a secret, who hadn't introduced him to her family and friends. So how could she expect him to include her with his family?

She logged into her email system and smiled when she saw a message from Jack.

'She walks in beauty, like the night, Of cloudless climes and starry skies.'

If anyone else saw it, they'd simply think that Jack and Miranda were having some sort of competition, vying for intellectual supremacy. They could even claim they were competing on a quiz for charity or something. No one would guess he was sending her something personal. Very personal.

A quick check in the poetry anthology she'd bought and secreted in her desk gave her the answer. She read the rest of the verse with a warm glow, then hit the reply button and typed, *Byron.*

It was a game. And yet it was serious—the equivalent to a love note. A coded message which told her how he felt about her.

And which brought home to her how she felt about him.

She stared at the screen. The last time she'd thought herself in love, it had all gone horribly, horribly wrong. She rubbed the ring finger on her left hand. She could still remember how it had felt, her finger missing the tiny weight of Rupert's engagement ring for weeks after she'd returned it.

It wasn't going to be like that with Jack. He wasn't Rupert. Her father had no idea what was happening. And Jack hadn't asked her to marry him.

But what if he did? What would she say? If she said yes, she ran the risk of everything collapsing round her ears again, the way it had with Rupert. And if she said no…the world would end. Either way, she lost.

She could feel her heart beating faster, the adrenaline running through her veins in response to panic. 'Enough,' she said loudly. 'It hasn't happened. It isn't going to happen.'

'What isn't?' Jack asked, leaning against the doorframe.

'Er…nothing. Just babbling to myself.'

'Everything OK?'

'Uh-huh.'

'Got a new one for you.' He gave her the slow, sweet smile that always speeded up her pulse rate. 'Elizabeth Barrett Browning, *Sonnets from the Portuguese*—number forty-three, line two plus half of line three.' He winked, and left the room.

The second he left, she whipped out the anthology. The poem wasn't there. She ended up nipping into the centre of Calderford in her lunch-break to look it up in the library. What she read sent a tremor down her spine. *'I love thee to the depth, breadth and height My soul can reach.'*

He loved her.

He loved her.

What was she going to do?

When Miranda got back to the ward—after a long walk that had done nothing to clear her head—she found Jack staring at an X-ray. 'Got a minute?' he asked.

How could he be so calm, so cool on the ward—when he'd just told her that he loved her? 'Sure,' she mumbled.

'Freya Brunning, aged fifty-seven. Presented with chest pain and palpitations, hacking cough—and a history of recurrent chest infections, breathing difficulties and malar flush.'

'Hmm.' A malar flush meant high colour over the cheekbones with a slightly bluish tinge, and could be a sign of mitral stenosis or narrowing of one of the heart's valves. On the other hand, she knew it wasn't always present in cases of mitral stenosis, and plenty of people had a high colour without heart disease. 'What does her chest sound like?'

'The apex beat's tapping, and when she lies on her left side and breathes out, there's a rumbling mid-diastolic murmur,' Jack said. 'She can't remember being ill but if it was ten, twenty years ago, she might not remember having rheumatic fever.'

The classic history of mitral stenosis was rheumatic fever, then ten years later the development of a heart murmur, then another ten years before the patient started developing symptoms, and another ten before the symptoms became really severe. Four times as many women as men were affected.

'I'm pretty sure we're talking mitral stenosis so I sent her for a chest X-ray.' He indicated the film he'd been looking at.

'Textbook example,' she said as she looked at the film. 'Left atrial enlargement, pulmonary oedema and the mitral valve's calcified.'

'Are we going straight for valve replacement, or shall we try drugs first?'

The question was left in the balance when Leila came over to them. 'Freya's in AF. And she's tachy.'

Tachycardia—a fast heartbeat—plus atrial fibrillation spelled trouble. 'We'll give her digoxin,' Miranda directed. 'And she'll need a beta-blocker because we need to keep her pulse rate below ninety. We'll write her up for warfarin as well—she really doesn't need the extra complication of a thrombosis or embolism.' Freya's age and the fact she had AF put her at a greater risk of developing a large blood clot that could end up blocking an artery. 'We'll keep her in for a few days for obs. If there's no real improvement, we're looking at surgery—probably valve replacement.'

She hadn't said a word to him, Jack thought as he walked up the steps to Miranda's flat that evening. Not a single word. No email, no text message, no sticky note, no cryptic comment—nothing.

It could be that she hadn't found the poem yet.

Or maybe she had—and he'd scared her off.

He was scared enough himself. He'd fallen for her so hard and so fast it terrified him. He fumbled with the box in his pocket. Last time he'd done this, it had all gone so horribly wrong. But this was different. Then he'd been a medical student, the engagement ring had been cheap and the girl he'd been in love with had been completely wrong for him. Now he was a man. The ring wasn't an engagement ring. Miranda wasn't going to be giggling with her friends about him. And he knew in his bones that she was the right one for him.

The problem was, he wasn't sure if she knew that, too.

"'Faint heart never won fair lady'',' he said wryly. He had to give it a try.

He rang her doorbell.

Even in faded jeans and a baggy T-shirt, she took his breath away. 'Hello, beautiful,' he said.

She leaned forward and kissed him. In the doorway, where anyone might see. Well, anyone walking up the stairs, he amended, which wasn't very likely. But it gave him renewed hope.

'Did you get the Barrett Browning?' Jack asked when she led him into the living room.

Miranda nodded.

'And?'

Her mouth went dry, to the point where she couldn't speak.

'You're panicking,' he said softly, capturing her chin between his thumb and forefinger and looking her straight in the eye. 'What's so scary about it?'

Because the last man who said he loved me broke my heart, Miranda thought.

He sighed when she didn't answer him. 'I thought we were doing the precipice thing together?'

'Yeah. I...um...'

'Miranda.' He sat down and pulled her onto his lap. 'It's been a month. I know how I feel about you—and I think you feel something for me, too.'

'I do.' But if she told him she loved him, it would all go wrong. Horribly, horribly wrong.

'Then isn't it time we went public?'

'No!'

He sighed. 'OK. I won't push you until you're ready.' He dropped a kiss on the end of her nose. 'Go have a shower. We'll go out for a Chinese.'

'Peking duck at the Willow Garden?' she asked.

'Sounds good. And if anyone spots us, I'll say it's a working dinner and we're discussing the trial we're starting next month.'

She nodded. 'I'll be five minutes.'

'I know your "five minutes",' he teased. 'I'll make some coffee.'

So far, so bad, Jack thought as Miranda disappeared into the bathroom. She still wouldn't acknowledge him publicly as her lover. Or tell him she loved him. The best she could say was that she 'felt something for him'—and that had been like pulling teeth, getting her to admit it.

Either she'd been so badly hurt that it would take a long while to build up her trust, or she wasn't serious about him. But in Glasgow no man had lasted more than two dates, and they'd been together for a whole month. Maybe there was hope for him. Maybe he just had to take it more slowly.

He took the box from his pocket, slipped it under her pillow, then went to make the coffee. By the time Miranda reappeared, having changed into smart trousers and a silk shirt, he was on his second cup of coffee. 'Any left for me?' she asked.

'No. I'll make some more.'

She shook her head and took the mug from him. 'I'll share yours.' She deliberately turned the mug to take a sip from the same place his lips had touched.

'Carry on like that,' he said softly, 'and it'll have to be a take-away.'

'You promised me Peking duck,' she reminded him. She tipped the rest of the coffee down the sink. 'And I'm hungry.'

Me, too. But I'm hungrier for you, Jack thought.

She was quiet during their meal out. And he realised with a sinking heart that he'd pushed her too far, too soon. He needed to backtrack. Now. So when he drove her home, he kissed her goodnight outside her front door.

'I'll see you tomorrow,' he said.

'But…' The question was written all over her face. *Why aren't you coming in?*

'You need space,' he said. 'I'll see you in the morning,' Gently, he brushed her lower lip with the pad of his thumb and left. Walking away from her was one of the hardest things he'd ever had to do—but he knew he had to do it.

The flat echoed. It felt *wrong* without Jack here. She padded around, unable to settle to anything. She couldn't relax to music—everything she picked out reminded her of him and time they'd spent together. She couldn't relax in the kitchen—she kept seeing him there, remembering the time they'd cooked a meal together and ended up burning everything because they'd been unable to keep their hands off each other. The bathroom, too, held memories. And the bedroom was unthinkable.

Space. He said he was giving her space. Or was he giving her an ultimatum? Go public, or go back to being colleagues only?

Hell. Hell and double hell.

She rummaged in the fridge for her chocolate supplies—but the box brought back too many memories. Jack had bought the praline hearts for her and had fed three of them to her before they'd ended up making love.

In the end she picked up the phone. It rang once, twice. 'Hello, you've reached Jack. Sorry I'm not here right now. Leave a message after the beep and I'll call you back.'

She could have cried. Or maybe he wasn't back yet. She hung up.

Thirty seconds later, her phone rang.

She ignored it. It wouldn't be him, would it? And if it was her father, nagging her about work, or her mother, nagging her about the charity party she'd organised and wanted Miranda to attend… She wasn't in the mood for dealing with either of them.

Her answering-machine beeped. 'Answering-machines are there to take messages, Ms Turner.' The speaker on her answering machine wasn't brilliant so she couldn't tell whether Jack was annoyed or teasing her. 'Or if you're going to chicken out of leaving a message, try withholding your number before you dial.' No, it was amusement. Definitely amusement. 'Pick up the phone, honey,' he said softly. 'I know you're there.'

There was a lump in her throat the size of a continent. She picked up the receiver. 'Hi,' she croaked.

'Hi, yourself.'

Why had he left the ball in her court? She was trying to think up a smart remark but, to her horror, a sob came out instead.

'What's the matter, honey?' he asked immediately.

Well, she was the one who believed in straight talking. And he'd been straight enough with her. She owed him. 'I'm miserable without you,' she said. 'I miss you.'

'Good.'

Good? This was where he was supposed to be all comforting and kind! How could he just say, 'Good'? She wanted to yell at him, but she couldn't. 'It just doesn't feel right without you here,' she muttered.

'Anything else you want to say to me?'

Miranda knew what he wanted to hear. All she had to do was say it. Say it. *Say* it. The seconds dragged on and on and on. Finally, she croaked, 'I love you.'

His voice softened immediately. 'Where are you?'

'In the living room.'

'Have you been in your bedroom yet?'

She frowned. Why was he asking her? 'No.'

'Go to bed,' he told her. 'Take the phone with you. I'll ring you in ten minutes.' And then he hung up.

Was he expecting her to have some kind of sexy phone conversation with him? Hell. She wanted him *here*. She wanted to be in his arms. Now. Held safe and close and warm. She'd admitted she missed him—she'd even admitted that she loved him. So why wasn't he coming over? Why wasn't he asking her to go to his place? Why had he told her to go to bed?

Men, she thought with a growl. She undressed, cleaned her teeth and then took the cordless phone into her bedroom.

She flung herself onto the bed, then shifted as she felt something hard beneath her head. She rummaged under the pillow and withdrew a small box wrapped in matt silver paper and decorated with curled ribbons. Her heart skipped a beat. No. Please, no. Please, don't let him have left her an engagement ring.

Then she looked at the box again. It was bigger than a normal-sized ring box. And, anyway, Jack hadn't said the four killer words. With trembling fingers she undid it. And gasped as she saw what was in the box. A navel ring in white gold, with a delicate purple rose that fitted in her navel.

On cue, the phone rang. She snatched it up. 'Hello?'

'It's me. Where are you?'

'In bed.'

'And?'

'It's beautiful,' she said, looking at the ring and the leaflet that had come with it. 'I'd never heard of purple gold before.'

'It's an alloy of gold and aluminium,' he said. 'Very new. I just thought it would be…very you.'

'Mmm. I'll wear it to work tomorrow.'

'Going to show me?'

'At work?'

'Yep. It's a date in the linen cupboard, yes?'

She paused. 'In other words, you want me to go public.'

'Yes. You're my girl, I love you and I want to show you off to the world.'

'Jack,' she said softly, 'I've told you I love you. But…I'm not ready for the world yet.' More specifically, she wasn't ready for her father. She had to figure out a way of seeing Jack without her father interfering and making another Rupert situation.

'So you're mine in private or not at all?'

'It's not *you*. It's me.'

'Isn't that what people say when they're trying to dump you nicely?'

'I'm not trying to dump you, Jack. Oh, hell. Stay where you are. Don't move,' she said.

Twenty minutes later, Jack heard the doorbell go. And go. And go. When he opened the door, Miranda was leaning on the doorbell. She marched in and stood facing him with her hands on her hips. 'I need an answer,' she said. 'Did you have it specially commissioned?'

'Why?'

'Don't play games.'

'OK. Yes, I did.'

'For me.'

'Uh-huh. Brian's sister-in-law is a jewellery designer.'

Her eyes narrowed. 'So your family knows about me?'

'No. I swore Sonia to secrecy.' What he didn't tell her was the condition of Sonia's promise—that they'd ask her to design their wedding rings. He had a feeling that now wouldn't be a good time to talk about other rings.

'Right.' She handed him a box.

Jack's eyes widened. It was the box he'd given her. Yes, now definitely *wasn't* the right time to mention other sorts of rings. Had he pushed her so hard she'd rejected his present?

'Aren't you going to open it?'

'No point. I know what's in it.'

'Do you?' She pulled up her T-shirt to bare her midriff. She was wearing his ring, the delicate purple rose sitting snugly in her navel.

So what was in the box?

'Open it,' she said softly.

He did. It contained a key. Was it what he thought it was—what he *hoped* it was? There was only one way to find out. 'And this is the key to…?'

'My front door.'

His heart skipped a beat. 'Are you asking me to move in with you?'

'I'm not sure,' she admitted. 'It's kind of…my way of telling you I trust you. And asking you to trust me.'

'Buying yourself some time?'

'Yes. Now shut up and kiss me.'

He grinned. 'I thought you'd never ask.'

The next morning, they were both on early. Usually Miranda left before he did, so they didn't arrive at the hospital together. For once, she didn't. She walked in with him. Not holding hands, as he would have liked, but at least she was with him. And her front door key nestled next to his on his keyring. The knowledge gave him a warm, fuzzy glow inside.

The night sister ran down the patient list with them both. 'Freya's still complaining of chest pain,' she finished.

'Right.' Miranda looked at Jack. 'Better give her an echo.'

'And measure the mitral valve opening,' he added. 'If it's less than two cubic centimetres—'

'Then we're talking valve replacement,' she said. 'Has Freya had anything to eat today?'

'Not yet,' the sister said.

'Good. Keep her nil by mouth and I'll prime Theatre.'

The echo showed exactly what they'd both feared—the mitral valve opening, which was usually around four to six square centimetres, was down to one and a half.

Miranda managed to book a late slot and she and Jack performed the valve replacement. By the time they'd finished, Miranda's shoulders ached. 'All that stitching,' she said.

Jack leaned closer. 'I'll give you a massage when we get home,' he murmured.

She smiled. 'I'll take a rain check on that. I need to stay late tonight in case there's a leakage in the valve replacement. And there's a risk of a bleed, too, from the anticoagulants we've given Freya.'

He glanced at his watch. 'There won't be anything decent left in the canteen at this time of night. Want me to get you a take-away and bring it up to your office?'

She shook her head. 'I'm too tired to eat.'

'I'll cook you something when you get in.'

'Maybe.' She gave him a tired smile. 'See you at home.'

Home. Such a simple little word, but it meant the world to him. Slowly but surely, she was letting him into her life. Into her heart.

CHAPTER NINE

'Miranda. You *still* haven't called me,' a cross voice announced on the tape. 'Now, I need to know. Are you going to bring a guest, or come on your own?'

Miranda pulled a face at her answering-machine. 'What happened to the third option, not going at all?' she asked as a beep signalled the end of the message. 'I hate these charity dos. Smiling at people and being pleasant in the hope they'll give tons of money to a good cause—even if I can't stand them.'

'You don't have to go,' Jack said. 'Just tell her you don't want to go. Give her the price of your ticket. I'll cough up, too, if you like. She won't say no to double funds.'

Miranda shook her head. 'I can't get out of it, Jack. If I throw a sickie, she'll know and I'll never hear the end of it. She has a nose for these things. I have to go.' She grimaced. 'And she's probably got some nice young man lined up to escort me. Or, if not to escort me, at least stick to me like glue during the do.' She sighed. 'I just wish my mother would realise that there's no point in matchmaking. The sort of men she picks for me are...well, they've got no soul, no sense of fun and they're all obsessed with having a bigger car and a higher salary and a larger house within the next three years. That's not what I want.'

So, what *did* she want? He didn't dare ask her. Just in case he didn't like the answer. 'You believe in straight talking. Tell her it's not your sort of thing.'

She rolled her eyes. 'You don't know my mother. She'll go straight into nag mode and she won't stop until I've agreed to go and do the dutiful daughter bit. There's this unofficial competition between her and the vice-chair to see who can organise events that raise the most money during the year. And my mother doesn't like to lose.' She gave Jack a speculative look. 'Are you busy on Thursday night?'

'I was planning a bit of stargazing.'

'How about stargazing in my parents' back garden?' she asked.

He stared at her. 'You want *me* to go to the do with you?'

'Uh-huh.'

How could he? He didn't fit in to that world. And then a seriously nasty thought struck him. Jessica's family probably moved in the same social circle as Miranda's. Supposing Jessica was there? Well, if she was, he'd just have to face it. Miranda needed him—and she was more important.

'So you're going to abandon me to it?'

Jack regained his grip. 'Define "with you".'

She rolled her eyes. 'How do you think? We go together.'

'You know what I mean. As colleagues—or as partners?'

He didn't understand the look on her face. Pain, mixed with fear. As if she was reliving an old and very nasty memory. 'When we go public, Jack, it'll be on our terms,' she said eventually. 'Not my mother's.'

'So as your colleague, then.'

'Do you mind? You're my number two on the ward. You're an obvious choice as my partner for the evening.'

I'm your *partner* partner, Jack wanted to argue. But he

knew there was no point. She'd already made her mind up. If he pushed her to let him go as her life partner, he'd lose her.

Hell. Why did she have to be so damned stubborn about it?

The next morning saw Jack studying an echocardiogram and an ECG strip.

'Penny for them?' Miranda said, noticing the frown on his face as she passed his desk.

'Take a look at this.' He passed her the echo.

She frowned. 'Clear.'

'No signs of cardiomyopathy or valve defects, right?'

'Right.'

'Now look at this.' He passed her the ECG strip.

She studied it, then grabbed a ruler and measured it. 'Long QT syndrome?'

He nodded grimly. It wasn't particularly common—the condition affected around one in ten thousand people—but with LQT syndrome the interval between the Q and T wave on the patient's ECG was longer than that in a normal heartbeat cycle, meaning that the heart's rhythm was disturbed.

'What's the family history?' she asked.

'Dad died young of a heart attack. Twin brother died last month. Luckily the GP was on the ball and sent Simon in for a check-up.'

'How old is he?'

'Nineteen. I'm just about to explain his test results to him.'

Miranda nodded. 'Give me a shout if you need me. Want to use my office? It's probably quieter than the day room. More private, anyway, when you're breaking bad news.'

'Thanks.' Jack took a deep breath and went to the day room. 'Sorry to have kept you waiting, Simon, Mrs Lane,' he said to the nineteen-year-old and his mother. 'Would you like to come through with me?'

When they were seated in Miranda's office with a cup of coffee, Jack talked them through the results. 'I do need to ask you one thing. How's your hearing, Simon?'

'Fine.'

'Any family history of deafness?'

Mrs Lane shook her head. 'Not on either side.'

So that ruled out the Jervell and Lange-Neilsen form of the condition, Jack thought, which meant Simon had the most common variant, known as Romano-Ward. 'What you've got is something called Long QT syndrome. It's an inherited disorder of your heart's electrical system, and it means your heart's rhythm is disturbed. Have you blacked out at all?'

'A few times,' Simon admitted. 'But I thought it was because I was overdoing it or...' he shot a glance at his mother '...not eating properly.'

'No. Because your heart's rhythm isn't doing what it should do, your heart can't supply your brain with enough blood and oxygen—that's why you black out. It's pretty scary for anyone who's there because they won't be able to feel your pulse.' Jack checked his notes. 'You're a student at the moment, yes?'

'Law.' Simon smiled. 'Hopefully a barrister, like my dad.'

'What about your brother?' Jack asked gently.

Mrs Lane sighed. 'Steve was a trader in the City. He lived life in the fast lane. Always at parties and...well, you know what they're like. Too much to drink, probably drugs as well—he swore he never took them, but I suppose he just didn't want me to worry.' Her eyes glistened with tears. 'Luckily Simon's more sensible.'

'Right.' Jack felt worse and worse. 'There's a very good chance that they both had the same condition.'

'Because they're twins?'

'Because it's an inherited condition. Do you have any other children, Mrs Lane?'

'A daughter, Sophie.'

'She really ought to have an ECG and an echo, so we can check whether she has the same condition,' Jack said gently. 'I'll book an appointment.'

'Thank you.' She sniffed. 'So what does it mean for my son?'

'It means that Simon needs a quiet life,' he said. 'I'm sorry to bring this up, but there is a risk of sudden death—it's possibly what happened to Simon's brother and father. The heart rhythm problem can be brought on by anything that stimulates adrenaline—exercise, emotion, loud noise. Even swimming.'

'So being a barrister's out?' Simon asked.

'If it means you're going to be flooded with adrenaline every time you step into court, yes,' Jack said. 'And I definitely don't advise competitive sports.'

Simon's eyes widened. 'So that's it? My career's down the toilet before I've even started, and I'm under a death sentence?'

'No. We can give you drugs to keep your condition under control—they're called beta-blockers and what they do is slow your heart rate and reduce the force of your heart's contractions. You'll need to be on them for the rest of your life, and I'll want to see you every six months for a check-up.' He looked at Simon. 'It's important that you take them.'

'Otherwise I'll die?'

'Otherwise you'll have a heart attack, and we might not be able to bring you back.' Particularly if he went into polymorphic VT, an irregular rhythm of the heart known as *torsade de pointes*. 'I'm sorry.'

'But if he takes the beta-blockers, he'll be all right?' Mrs Lane asked.

'And avoids stressful situations.'

Simon gave the glimmer of a smile. 'In other words, be a couch potato.'

'I wouldn't go that far,' Jack said, smiling back. 'Just keep the exercise very, very gentle.'

On Thursday evening, Jack made them both a coffee and wrestled with his bow-tie while Miranda finished dressing.

She walked into the kitchen and stopped dead. 'Wow.' Her lips quirked. 'I'm tempted to ring my mother and tell her I've got other plans.'

'Such as?'

'Stripping all that lot off you again.'

'Don't you dare.' He pulled a face at her. 'I've spent ages sorting out this wretched tie.'

'You should've asked me.'

She'd probably learned to do a proper bow-tie when she'd still been in her pram, he thought wryly. 'You look pretty good, too.' In a classic little black dress and high heels, with her hair down. She wore a single strand of pearls—real ones, he guessed—plus matching earrings, and that was the only jewellery she wore.

As if she'd read his mind—or maybe it showed on his face—she took his hand. 'Only the boring jewellery's on show. Two people—well, three, if you count your designer friend—know about the most important piece.'

So she was wearing his ring. Was that supposed to

make him feel better? It didn't. He felt ill at ease, out of his depth, in a way he never did at work.

The feeling got worse as the evening wore on, because the party was everything Miranda had said it would be. The marquee was set up in a back garden that had more square footage than his house and his brothers' put together. The bar was selling champagne at exorbitant prices that everyone was happy to pay because the money was going to charity—he only got away with drinking orange juice because he claimed he was on call, and because he paid champagne prices for it. The band was playing ballroom dance music and he wasn't good at dancing anyway, much less something formal like this, whereas Miranda knew all the steps to all the dances and seemed to dance with just about everyone in the marquee.

The people were everything she'd said they'd be, too. The younger ones all spoke in braying voices, talking about their latest enormous deals or huge fee-paying cases. He lost count of how many times he was asked why he hadn't gone into private practice— 'Make a packet, old chap.' And the pitying looks he was given when he gave the honest reply, 'I went into medicine to help people, not to make my fortune.'

How could Miranda—warm, caring, brisk and efficient Miranda—come from a background like this? It was Jessica all over again, he thought with a sinking heart. Her parents and their circle would never accept him—he simply wasn't one of them. Miranda's mother had been terribly polite to him, but she'd clearly worked out within seconds that his dinner jacket was hired, then had decided it wasn't worth pursuing a matchmaking exercise. *Not the kind of man you'd marry.* Even now, years later, the thought made him flinch. With Jessica, he'd walked away. With Miranda…he'd do anything to make her happy. And if that meant learning to make the right noises, he'd just have to do it.

He was about to find Miranda and ask her how quickly they could disappear without upsetting her mother when he was cornered by a man in his sixties wearing a velvet smoking-jacket and matching bow-tie. The broken veins on his nose and cheeks hinted at a lifetime of drinking too much, a sign Jack knew only too well from his father.

'Sawyer, isn't it? Turner tells me you're the new up-and-coming hotshot at the hospital,' the old man said. 'Heart medicine, what?'

Jack forced a polite smile to his face. 'I work with Miranda.'

'Good show, good show.' The old man lifted his glass. 'Jolly good do.'

'Yes,' Jack said politely.

'Can't stand champagne myself.' He tapped his nose. 'Had a word with Milly. Sorted me out a nice single malt. Made me pay an arm and a leg, of course, but it's for charity. Have to do right by her.'

'Yes.' Jack's smile was becoming more and more fixed.

'Had a cleaner once called Sawyer, y'know. Felt sorry for her. Widow on her own, three boys to bring up. Husband died of drink.' The old man took another swig from his glass. 'Course, it was all a front.'

Ice slid down Jack's spine. He could have been describing Jack's mother—the same name, the same circumstances. Had this man been one of his mother's clients? Jack hadn't known any of them. But what did he mean, 'all a front'?

'Sob story. Probably none of it true. Well, she had the three nippers. Saw her meeting them from school. But…' He shook his head. 'Had to let her go.' What Jack assumed was meant to be a confidential whisper came out as more of a roar. 'Stealing, you know. Money from the wife's purse, the odd bit of jewellery.'

No. He surely couldn't mean *Jack's* mother. Jack knew she'd never stolen anything in her life!

'Haven't thought of her for years. Sawyer.' The old man leaned forward. 'Hmm, same eyes. Not related, are you?'

'You must be mistaken. My mother would never steal anything,' Jack said.

'No, no.' The old man waved his glass around. 'Co-incidence. Same name. Of course, your mother wouldn't be a cleaner. Wouldn't be a thief. Would she?'

The whole room seemed to have gone quiet. Jack knew without doubt that everyone was staring at them, having caught half the conversation.

'Actually, my mother *was* a cleaner,' he said. 'She supported me through medical school and I'm proud of her. But she wouldn't dream of stealing.'

The old man made a noise between a splutter and a laugh. 'This one did. Ask the wife. Cynthia? Cynthia?' he bellowed.

Miranda materialised next to Jack and slipped her arm through his. 'Hello, Les. Been at my father's malt, have we?'

'Just telling this young fellow—'

'I know,' she cut in. 'I heard. And you're mistaken. Jack's mother is a very nice woman.'

How would Miranda know? Jack thought. They'd never even met! Unless… Oh, no. Please, don't let his mother have cleaned for Miranda's family, too.

'She's not a thief. And Jack is very highly respected in the hospital.' She patted Les's hand. 'I think you need to take a little rest from this. Sit down, have a little nap.'

'But— No, this young man's saying I'm a liar.'

'He's saying you're mistaken,' Miranda said. 'And he's right.'

'No, no. She was a thief. Had to let her go. You ask Cynthia. Cynthia!' he bellowed. His colour rose alarmingly.

'Come and sit down, Les,' Miranda said soothingly. 'Let me take that glass for you.'

'I won't. I *won't* be called a liar. Cynthia!'

And then he dropped the glass. In what seemed like slow motion the glass tumbled over and over, the malt whisky splashing from it in droplets like treacle. The glass bounced once, twice—and then the old man hit the floor.

Miranda and Jack looked at each other. Jack immediately dropped to his knees, removed Les's bow-tie and loosened his collar.

Miranda grabbed the nearest person to them. 'Find my father. Tell him to get his bag from his study. Now,' Miranda said.

'And call an ambulance,' Jack added. 'No pulse, no respiration,' he said to Miranda. From the way Les had fallen, he wasn't likely to have a spinal injury. Quickly, Jack tilted Les's head back and checked his airways.

'Clear?' Miranda asked.

'Yep. I'll breathe, you do the compressions,' he said.

They swung into the old familiar rhythm of CPR, one breath to five compressions.

'We're not letting you go,' Jack said, as Miranda did the fifth set of compressions while he checked Les's pulse. 'Absolutely *not*.'

They continued the CPR. 'We have a pulse,' he said with relief.

Ralph arrived with his bag. 'What do you need?' he asked.

'Thrombolytics, if you have them,' Jack said.

'Sorry, no.' Ralph shook his head. 'Ambulance ETA five minutes. Is it an MI?'

'Probably. Which makes it number three, if I'm counting correctly,' Miranda said grimly. 'But if he won't give up cigars and whisky or eat sensibly, what does he expect?'

'Allow me the pleasure of giving him the lecture when we're back on the ward and he's stabilised,' Jack said, equally grimly.

'He's all yours,' Miranda promised. She looked up at her father. 'Don't you want to…?'

Ralph spread his hands. 'Apart from the fact that I've had two glasses of champagne, I hardly think I need to. Not with the consultant *and* the special reg from my cardiac ward in attendance. No, no, you carry on.'

'Right. Aspirin?' Miranda asked. The minute Les was able to sit up again, she'd give him the aspirin to chew— it would help the anti-clotting effect of the thrombolytic drugs he'd be given later.

Ralph handed her a foil strip of tablets. 'Anything else, or can I lock this up again?'

'That's it, thanks,' Jack said.

Fifteen minutes later, Les was in hospital and hooked up to an ECG monitor. Miranda stayed with him while Jack talked to Cynthia in Miranda's office, explaining what was going to happen next and what they needed to do.

'I feel so guilty,' Cynthia said. 'But I had to support Milly's do, and he wouldn't let me go on my own—he can't bear staying at home and resting.'

'He'll have to learn. Or try some relaxation therapies.'

'He says they're all a load of hokum.'

He *would*, Jack thought.

'I…um, heard him shouting for me.'

'Yes.'

'I don't know what it was about. Someone was saying something about a thief.'

As she'd brought it up… 'Actually, he was talking about your ex-cleaner. A Mrs Sawyer.'

'Shirley?'

Then it hadn't been coincidence. The chances of two widowed Mrs Sawyers with three children living in the same city were low enough. The chances of them both being called Shirley must be virtually zero. Jack's heart sank. It had to be a mistake. It *had* to. 'My mother's name is Shirley Sawyer. She worked as a cleaner when I was younger. I have no idea if you were one of the people she cleaned for. But she was never, ever a thief,' Jack said.

'I know.' Cynthia bit her lip. 'It was Chantal.'

'Chantal?'

'Our daughter. She'd got in with a bad crowd at school. I had a long talk with her, brought her to her senses and she stopped doing it—but she begged me not to tell her father. I knew Les would hit the roof if he found out the truth, so I said I'd dealt with it. It was around the same time as Shirley stopped doing for us, so I let him think…' Her voice trailed off as she looked at Jack, clearly realising the implications.

'You let him think my mother was a thief,' Jack said. 'I see.'

'I know, I know, it was an awful thing to do, and you've just saved his life, and—'

Cynthia looked as if she was about to start crying. Jack patted her hand. 'Now's not the time to discuss it. But I would appreciate it if you could clear my mother's name. Sooner, rather than later, please.'

'Yes, yes, I— He's a difficult man. Gets the bit between his teeth and runs away with it—he's always been like that.'

'And if he doesn't calm down, he's going to have another heart attack. Next time we might not be able to bring him back. When he's stabilised I'll be reading him the Riot Act. And you need to do your bit—get rid of the drink, get rid of the cigars and make sure your friends and family all know that if they indulge him on the quiet, they're as good as signing his death warrant,' Jack said. 'Come on. I'll take you to see him.'

When at last Miranda was sure Les was stable, she and Jack left the ward. They walked back down to his car in silence.

All the time, Miranda was trying to push the thoughts out of her head. But they refused to go away. Jack's father had been an alcoholic and had died of oesophageal varices. He had two brothers. He'd told her his mother had worked as a cleaner, done two jobs to clear his father's debts. *Had* she been a thief?

No. Of course not. Les must have got it wrong. And as far as Miranda was concerned, she couldn't care less if Jack's mother had been a thief. Jack was the important one.

But she knew that wasn't how her family would see it. She could imagine the gossip that was still going on back in the marquee. About how Les had rowed with the young doctor and then collapsed—and the row had been about the doctor's mother being a thief. Jack hadn't even had a chance to stay and defend his mother. He'd done what any doctor would have done—he'd stayed with his patient, despite the fact that his patient had thrown abuse at him.

Maybe they should go back and face the crowd. But Miranda had a nasty feeling that it would be a case of shutting the stable door after the horse had bolted. Way too late. Because the rumours would already have worked their way back to her mother. And Milly Turner had already guessed what was happening between Jack Sawyer and her daughter. Miranda knew that without her mother even having to say anything—she knew how observant Milly was. Milly wouldn't keep it from her husband either. And as soon as Ralph found out that Miranda was seeing the son of an alleged thief, he'd interfere—just as he had with Rupert. With a few words he'd make perfectly sure Jack stayed away from his daughter. He could wipe out Jack's career for ever. Miranda really, really couldn't let that happen.

So there was only one thing she could do to protect Jack.

When Jack parked outside her flat, Miranda sighed. 'I'm tired. I think I'll have an early night.'

'OK.'

'Thanks for dropping me home.'

So she didn't want him to come up? A tiny part of Jack's heart withered. 'So I'm going home on my own tonight?'

'I think that might be a good idea,' she said carefully.

His grip tightened on the steering-wheel. Oh, no. Please, no. Don't let this be the beginning of the end. She'd stood up for him at the party, but now she'd had time to think about Les's accusations. If you threw enough mud, some of it stuck. 'Look, Jack—I've been thinking.'

Here it came.

'We should cool it a bit. I mean, the past month—it's been amazing. But we work together. Things could get awkward.'

Especially if it leaked out that she was having a relationship with the son of an alleged thief—even though the allegations weren't true, people would still talk. 'As you wish.' Well, he wasn't going to beg her to change her mind. If she was really that shallow, she couldn't be the woman he'd fallen in love with. She was just another Jessica. And he'd never, ever make that mistake again. This time he'd really learned his lesson. He took the keys from the ignition and removed her front door key from his keyring. 'Perhaps you'd better have this back.'

She took it and swallowed nervously. 'I'd better give you your ri—'

'Keep it,' he cut in. 'I'll see you on the ward tomorrow, Ms Turner.'

For a moment he thought she was going to say something else. Then she climbed out of his car. He waited until she'd gone inside the apartment block, and then drove home. Funny, after Jessica he'd thought his heart had broken. Now he knew it hadn't. Because his heart had just crumbled into tiny pieces. And it could never be whole again.

Miranda closed her front door behind her then slid down, her back against the door, until she was sitting on the floor. She curled up into the foetal position, her arms wrapped round her knees and her head bowed. She knew how much she'd hurt Jack—but if she'd let things carry on between them, he'd have been hurt even more. Her father wouldn't hesitate to use the lies about Jack's mother to split them up, then ruin Jack's credibility at the hospital. Ruin his career. Ruin his future.

'Oh, Jack,' she said brokenly.

And then the tears came, scalding her eyes and searing into her soul.

CHAPTER TEN

MIRANDA was at her desk early the next morning. Jack barely spoke to her on the ward round and she noticed that he stayed well away from Les's room. Worse, he hardly spoke to anyone else on the ward either.

'All right, what have you done to him?' Leila asked, her hands on her hips and a grin on her face. 'Taken his toys away?'

Miranda's heat hammered. 'What do you mean?'

Leila gave her a strange look. 'Nothing. Just that Jack's in a funny mood and I wondered if you—as the boss—had any idea what's up.'

Every idea. 'Your guess is as good as mine,' Miranda said, hoping the ward sister wouldn't notice the evasion.

'Right.' Leila shrugged. 'I dare say he'll get over it.'

But he didn't. He even snapped at Hannah when she asked him if everything was all right, when he was usually patience personified with their student. And the tension between Jack and Miranda grew worse still over the next couple of days. Jack made a parcel of everything she'd left at his house and put it in the bottom drawer of her desk at work—without so much as a note. Then again, he probably thought they'd already said it all. There was nothing left to say.

She stayed out of his way as much as she could. But she was forced to work with him on the Tuesday.

'Patient history?' he asked.

If he wanted it short, that's the way he'd get it, she thought. 'Ebstein's anomaly.'

148

He said nothing, merely folded his arms.

Well, she'd given him the diagnosis, not the history. She sighed. 'Patty's sixteen. Tired all the time, breathlessness on exertion. Presented with cyanosis and signs of right heart failure—swollen ankles and ascites.' Ascites meant there was excess fluid between the membranes lining the abdominal wall. 'Her JVP and atrial pulses are normal but the first heart sound is widely split. Tricuspid regurgitation—oh, and her mother's a manic depressive, and apparently didn't realise she was pregnant until she was four months.'

'So she took lithium in the first trimester of pregnancy?'

The effect of the mood-stabilising drug on the foetus was one of the possible causes of Ebstein's anomaly. Miranda nodded. 'Patty's echo shows a dilated right ventricle and atrium. I've booked her in surgery for this afternoon to repair the tricuspid valve.' In Ebstein's anomaly, the tricuspid valve was further down the right ventricle than it should be, so it couldn't work properly.

'Fine.'

'I'm writing her up for diuretics, digoxin and ACE inhibitors.' ACE, or angiotensin-converting enzyme inhibitors, reduced the constriction of blood vessels, letting blood flow more easily through them and reducing blood pressure. They often reduced blood pressure so dramatically on the first dose that the patient was at risk of collapsing, so the drugs were usually given in a low dose under supervision in hospital. 'We'll book her in for regular check-ups and recommend a low-salt diet.'

'Fine.'

He was cool, calm and efficient throughout the operation, and Miranda wanted to scream. Where had her passionate lover gone?

But she was the one who'd sent him away. She had no one else to blame but herself.

'I hear you had two heroes at the party last night,' Ally said when she brought Ralph's coffee in.

The professor looked up from his paperwork. 'Heroes?'

'Your daughter and Jack,' Ally prompted. 'They saved someone's life.'

'Oh. Yes. They make a good team.'

'Don't they just?'

Something in her tone made Ralph frown. 'How do you mean?'

'Oh—er, they work well together,' Ally said, backtracking swiftly.

'That wasn't what you meant, was it?' Ralph asked.

'I…um, well, I don't want to repeat any gossip.'

Ralph waited. Ally was good at her job, and she kept an ear to the rumour machine. She'd helped him out several times before, telling him rumours that were circulating so he could step in when needed and limit any damage. He had a nasty feeling that this was going to be another such case.

'I don't want to get anyone into trouble,' she said.

'Are you saying that Jack Sawyer and my daughter are an item?'

She sucked her teeth. 'Um…well, they're close.'

'Outside work?'

'I really couldn't say, Professor.'

In other words, yes. Milly had said as much to him after the party—something about the way Miranda had looked at Jack—and he'd dismissed it, saying they were just colleagues. He sighed heavily. Clearly not, and the whole hospital was probably talking about it. 'And this rumour is doing the rounds, is it?'

'I think they tried to keep it quiet,' Ally said unhappily. 'Look…it could be worse. Jack's a decent bloke.'

'Indeed,' Ralph said, his voice crisp.

'I'm sure he'll treat her well.'

'Indeed,' Ralph said again.

Ally shifted uncomfortably. 'I don't want to get anyone into trouble.'

'You won't. But you could perhaps remind anyone who gossips that I prefer my staff not to have relationships with others on the same ward. When it ends, it can make life that little bit too awkward at work.'

'Of course, sir.'

When Ally had left, Ralph stared unseeingly at his papers. He'd been here before with Miranda. She'd chosen someone unsuitable, someone who… Well, never mind. He'd sorted that out. Hopefully Ally would pass on the word and hearing his views about mixing work and relationships would make Miranda see sense this time. Stop things before it was too late.

If it wasn't already too late.

Miranda was writing up notes when Leila tapped on her open door. 'Miranda? I need you for an admission.'

Why couldn't Jack do it?

The question must have been written on her face because Leila said softly, 'It's Jack's mum.'

'I'm there.' Miranda dropped her pen and went straight through to Room Four with the ward sister.

'Mrs Sawyer, this is Miranda Turner, the consultant,' Leila said.

'Call me Miranda,' Miranda said with a warm smile.

She glanced down at the notes. 'So you were at work when you felt a tightness round your chest?'

'I thought it was indigestion. It was Tracey's birthday at work so she'd bought cream cakes for everyone,' Shirley said. 'I couldn't be rude and say no, so I had one with my coffee. It didn't agree with me so I took some antacids. Then my arm started to hurt and I couldn't breathe properly. They rang the ambulance and they brought me here.'

'I'm going to do some tests to see if you've had a heart attack,' Miranda said. 'Does your chest hurt now?'

Shirley shook her head. 'They gave me some painkillers downstairs.'

'And gave you some oxygen in a mask?'

Shirley nodded.

'OK. Leila's going to take some blood from you, and I'm going to attach a monitor so we can see what your heart's doing. When I know a little bit more, I'll let Jack come and see you.'

'He's here?' Shirley's eyes brightened.

'On his break,' Leila said smoothly.

'Thanks. Keep him away for now,' Miranda mouthed, out of Shirley's sight. 'I'll break the news.'

When she'd finished sorting out all the tests and had confirmed from the ECG that Shirley had had a mild heart attack, she left Leila to observe and went to find Jack.

'Can we have a quick word in my office, please?'

He gave her a look that clearly said, *Do I have to?*, but he went with her.

'Sit down,' she said, and closed the door behind them. 'What's going on?'

'There isn't a nice way to say this.'

'Well, you're the expert at straight talking. You may as well spit it out.'

She flinched, but knew she'd deserved it. She'd hurt him badly. 'It's your mother,' she said. 'She's had a mild MI.'

'Where is she?'

'Hold on.' She put a hand on his shoulder to stop him storming out of the room to his mother's beside, then removed her hand when he glared at her. 'Jack, you *can't* treat her. She's your mother. It's against the rules to treat your own family, remember? But I'll answer any questions you have.'

'I'll be checking her notes.'

'Look, I know there are problems between us.' His eyes said, *And whose fault is that?* 'But I don't think you have a problem with my work—do you?'

'No,' he admitted.

That was a hurdle she could really do without right now. 'Good. I'll give your mother the best care in my ability, and I'll keep you informed at all times. If you need any time off work, just let me know and I'll organise a locum.'

'Right. Now, can I go and see my mother?'

'Yes.' Miranda didn't bother giving him the usual spiel about the patient being tired and needing to rest. He already knew it, so there was no point. She sighed and sat down behind her desk. Time to call in a few favours.

Jack didn't neglect his duties on the ward, she noticed. But he spent every break in his mother's room. And when his brothers arrived, wanting to know what had happened, Jack insisted on taking over and telling them.

It wasn't quite that she felt rejected. Just that…if things had been different, maybe she could have been there with them. Shared the hugs. Shared the obvious affection between them all.

If it had been her mother in there… Well, Milly would have sent Miranda on errands and virtually blackmailed her into taking over as much of the charity work as possible. Ralph would have visited, of course—but there would have been no warm hugs, no sitting holding hands, no gentle touches to show he understood she was worried but she didn't have to share the burden alone.

She could have had a family. *This* family. But she'd thrown it all away.

The following morning, Jack walked straight into Miranda's office without knocking. 'Where did that television come from?'

'What television?'

'The touch-screen job in my mother's room.'

'Oh. That.'

'And the menu card she gave me isn't the one everyone else on the ward is using.'

'Um, no. Sorry, I meant to collect that earlier.'

'What are you up to?'

She spread her hands. 'OK. I confess. I borrowed the TV from Pasteur Ward.'

'The private ward.' His lips thinned. 'And the menu card just happens to be the same as the one for private patients. Are you going to tell me this is a coincidence?'

'Jack, calm down.'

'Charlie and Brian didn't organise private treatment, and I didn't either. So what's going on?'

'Your mother's not having private treatment exactly. Just some of the, um, comforts. I called in a few favours.'

His eyes narrowed. 'Don't you dare patronise me, Miranda. Not now.'

'I'm not.' She shook her head in frustration. 'Look, she's your *mother*. If any family member of *any* of my staff came onto this ward, I'd do the same thing. Call it what you like—staff perks, whatever.'

A muscle tightened in his jaw. Clearly he didn't believe her. 'I'll pick up the bill.'

'There isn't one.'

'I *said*,' he informed her crisply, his voice all the more scary because it was so quiet and measured, 'I'll pay for it. My family doesn't take favours. My family doesn't take, full stop.'

'Jack, I—'

But he'd already left.

Later that day, when Jack was busy with another patient, Miranda went to check on Shirley.

'How are you feeling?' she asked softly.

'A bit tired. But thank you, love. You've been kind.'

'Any time.'

'You're the one, aren't you?'

Miranda frowned. 'Sorry, I don't follow you.'

'You're the one who put the smile back behind my son's eyes. For a little while.'

Miranda flushed. 'Um… He told you about me?'

Shirley shook her head. 'I guessed. He never tells me anything about himself outside work. Not since Jessica.'

Who was Jessica? What had she meant to Jack? Why hadn't he told Miranda anything about her? She tried to push back the flood of jealous questions. She didn't have a right to be jealous. Not any more.

'He didn't tell you about her.' It was a statement, not a question.

'What happened?'

Shirley looked sad. 'I don't know much. Just that she

hurt him very badly. Since her, Jack just clams up about his personal life. It's worse than pulling teeth, getting information out of him. So I end up nagging him and pushing him, and fussing too much. I know he needs space, but I just want to get through to him and it drives me crazy that he's so *difficult* about it. He's a fantastic uncle and he'll make a brilliant father...' She smiled wryly. 'But you know all that, don't you?'

'Yes.' Miranda dug her nails into her palm. She knew all that, and still she'd let him walk out of her life.

'For a while he seemed happier than I could remember. He didn't say anything to me about it but I guessed he was in love.' Shirley paused. 'He does love you, you know. And I've seen the way you look at him.'

Miranda went straight into panic mode. Was it so obvious? Or was it just because Shirley was Jack's mum that she'd noticed?

'You love him, don't you?' Shirley asked.

'That's a question I'd rather not answer, if you don't mind,' Miranda said carefully.

'What went wrong?' Before Miranda had a chance to think up a suitable reply, Shirley sighed. 'No, there's no point in even asking you, pet. You're not going to tell me either, are you?'

'It's complicated.'

'Is it something you can work through together?'

No. Most definitely not. Jack would never listen to her again—and she could hardly blame him. She changed the subject. 'You,' Miranda told her gently, 'are supposed to be resting, Shirley Sawyer. And your son will have my guts for garters if he thinks I'm worrying you. I'll see you later, OK?'

Work. She had to concentrate on work. It was the only way she was going to get through these weeks. Forcing back the tears, she went to Les's room to check on him. 'How are you feeling?'

'Guilty,' he said. 'Owe that young doctor an apology. Cynthia, um, put me in the picture. Thief wasn't his mother.' He rolled his eyes. 'That daughter of ours. In with a bad crowd. I should have—'

'Hey,' she cut in. 'Don't start getting worked up. You'll make yourself ill again.'

'Would you send him in to see me? I understand why he doesn't want anything to do with me, but I need to tell him I know the truth. Need to *apologise*.' Les's face twisted. 'Made a real fool of myself.'

'Les,' she said quietly, 'Jack's got other things on his mind at the moment.' She crossed her fingers. This wasn't *really* breaking patient confidentiality. 'His mum's in here, too.'

Les's face went white. 'Because of me and what I said?'

'No, not because of you.'

'I owe her an apology, too. I've been such a—such a—'

'Hothead?' she finished wryly. 'Les, you always were.'

'Can I see her?'

'Not right now,' she said.

'Soon. Before you let me out of here. Please?'

'We'll see.'

'You're a bossy young madam,' Les said. 'Just like your mother.'

Miranda smiled. 'I'll take that as a compliment.'

The next day, Miranda called Jack into her office again.

He stood there, unsmiling, waiting for her to say her piece.

'Les wants to see you.'

'I'm busy.'

'He wants to apologise, Jack. He knows now that your mother wasn't a thief.'

'Which is what I said all along.'

'I never, ever believed your mother was a thief.'

'Don't tell me—she used to clean for your family, too?' he asked nastily. 'Is that how you knew she was a "very nice woman"?'

'No, she didn't—the first time I met her was when she came onto the ward. I knew she was nice because she was *your* mother. And only…' She stopped, aware that she was digging herself a hole. Only a very nice woman could have produced a son as kind, caring and thoughtful as Jack. A man she'd walked away from. 'Les told me the thief was his daughter, who'd got in with a bad crowd.'

'And that's supposed to make everything all right?'

'He wants to apologise, Jack. It's worrying him, and that's going to set back his recovery. And he wants to see your mother, too.'

'Absolutely not,' Jack said. 'I don't want her dragged into this mess.'

'And if she finds out later what's happened?'

'She won't find out anything from me. Now, if you've finished?'

Miranda gave up and let him go. But she noticed later that he checked on Les, and spent a while talking to the old man. At least they'd made their peace. She'd just have to live with the fact that she and Jack would never be able to make theirs. Maybe one day it'd be easy to work with him again. Maybe one day she'd be able to look at him without remembering how it had felt to wake up in his arms. Maybe. Until then, she had no choice.

CHAPTER ELEVEN

MIRANDA spent a miserable Sunday on her own. How on earth had she spent the last few years being smug about being gloriously independent and not having to please anyone else because she had her own space? It wasn't like that any more. It was just…lonely. Unbearably lonely, now she knew what it was like to have that space filled with a gorgeous, funny, caring man. One who'd teased her and taught her to enjoy the simple pleasures. One who'd made her feel warm and *loved*. He'd even said he loved her. *'To the depth, breadth and height My soul can reach.'*

And she'd thrown it all away.

She stayed out of Jack's way at work. Stayed out of his way when both Les and Shirley went down to the general men's and women's wards respectively. Stayed out of his way—until one Tuesday morning when she came on duty on a late and saw him studying an X-ray film. His shoulders were absolutely rigid and the tension was coming off him in waves. Something was obviously very wrong.

She wanted to rush over and put her arms round him. She wanted to hold him, tell him it was all going to be OK. But she didn't have that right any more—and she wasn't going to risk a very public rejection. There was only one approach she could take. That of his boss.

'Problem?' she asked lightly, coming to stand beside him.

'Nothing I can't handle,' he rapped back.

'I didn't say it was,' she said coolly. 'But I've just come on duty, so I'd like an update on the ward.'

'Ask Leila.'

Whatever it was, it had seriously rattled him. Jack had *never* been rude to her like this on the ward, no matter how bad things were between them personally. 'Can we have a word in my office, please?' She spoke quietly, but it wasn't a request. And, from the look on his face, he knew it.

She closed the door behind him and leaned against it. 'Right. Let's get this very clear, shall we? You and I aren't getting on well at the moment.' That was an understatement, and she knew it, but it was the only neutral way she could think of to put it. 'But we need to make sure the patients don't suffer. Their needs have to come first—so, no matter how angry you are with me, you leave our differences outside the ward. Clear?'

He gave her a mocking salute. 'Yes, ma'am. No, ma'am. Three bags full, ma'am.'

She gritted her teeth. 'Look, I know you're angry with me.'

'Angry?' He looked scornfully at her.

She folded her arms. 'And it's to do with Jessica.'

His eyes narrowed. 'What do you mean, Jessica?'

'You know exactly what I mean.' She was bluffing—but it was the only way she was going to get the truth out of him. She just hoped he didn't realise she was bluffing.

'What did my mother tell you?'

'I can't break a confidence.' She flung his own words back at him.

'If you know so much, Ms Clever-Clogs, then you don't need to ask.'

One spectacular own goal. She sighed. 'Actually, she

didn't tell me much at all. I was guessing. Look, I've apologised. What do you expect me to do—crawl over broken glass? Wear a hair shirt? Fast for a month?'

'Don't be ridiculous.'

Her temper snapped at his scorn. 'Whether you like it or not, we have to work together. For the sake of our patients and everyone else on the team, we have to get on. You might hate me, but you'll just have to swallow it until we're off the ward. If you want a fight, sure, you can have one. With pleasure.' Right now she wanted to throttle him. 'But *not* on the ward.'

'And what did I do wrong?' Jack asked. His voice faded so she could barely hear him. 'Besides being stupid enough to say I loved you.'

'Nothing.' Her anger dissolved. 'It's not you. It's me.'

He gave a short, mocking laugh. 'Oh, spare me. That's what nice girls say when they dump you. To stop themselves feeling guilty.'

It wasn't like that. But she couldn't explain—not without telling him all about what had happened with Rupert. And it was way too late for that. 'We have to work together. So let's make a truce on the ward.'

'A truce.'

'A truce,' she repeated.

There was a long, long silence. But eventually he nodded. 'On the ward.'

'Right. So—your patient?'

'Skip Jones, aged fifty-three. Dilated cardiomyopathy.'

Dilated cardiomyopathy—a disease of the heart muscle where the walls of the heart ballooned out—was linked to alcohol abuse. No wonder Jack was tense. Thinking of his father, no doubt.

'Presentation?' she asked, wanting to know the symptoms Skip had complained about.

'The usual. Fatigue, breathlessness—especially at night—occasional palpitations, and coughing up pink frothy sputum. I think we're looking at left ventricular failure.'

'Pulse?'

'Up. So's his JVP, though his blood pressure's down.'

'What about the chest X-ray?'

Jack tapped Skip's file. 'It's here, if you want to see it. It shows prominent upper lobe vessels and an enlarged heart. There's pleural effusion—' meaning fluid in the chest cavity '—and oedema. Textbook example—you know, bat's wings shadowing and Kerley B lines.' These were opaque lines on the X-ray films showing interstitial oedema or fluid in the deep tissues. 'Hannah ought to see it.'

'Have you asked about—' she knew this was going to hurt him, but she had to ask, for the patient's sake '—his drinking?'

Jack nodded. 'Red wine. A couple of bottles a day. For—oh, twenty years or so. He owns an advertising agency and lives up to the stereotype, wining and dining his clients. Has a liquid lunch, then out in the evenings for dinner and more of the same. Oh, and that doesn't include the pre-dinner gins.'

'Have you done an echo?'

'Yep. It's what you'd expect. Pulmonary hypertension, mitral and tricuspid valve regurgitation, all four chambers of the heart dilated.'

'Do you want me to do this?' she asked.

'No. I can cope.'

'You don't have to prove anything.'

He gave her a withering look. 'What makes you think I'm trying to prove anything?'

'So much for our truce,' she muttered.

'I'm sorry. And you're right, yes, it's bringing back memories. But I have to face them some time,' Jack said. 'Anyway, my treatment plan. The alcohol has to stop as of now—and I'll make it clear to him that if he starts drinking again, he's going to die. Full stop. I'm putting him on bed rest, diuretics and observations for a while. If that doesn't help, I'll try ACE inhibitors, provided his blood results don't contraindicate it. When his blood results come back, I'll check his electrolytes. If there's anything abnormal I'll get them corrected so he doesn't go into arrhythmia.'

'What about vitamin supplements?' she asked.

'Thiamine, B12 and folate.'

'OK.'

Walking away from her was hard. All he wanted to do was hold her—hold her, and feel her arms round him. Ah, hell. One day he'd wake up and stop missing her. Stop wanting to be with her. But no way was he going to put himself back in a situation where she could reject him again as the mood took her.

He busied himself taking Hannah through the finer points of chest X-rays and ECG traces. 'Good. You've remembered a lot,' he said when he'd finished testing the student on the heart waves he'd taken her through a few days before.

She flushed pink with pleasure. 'Thanks to your help. Um, Jack, I was wondering…would you like to come out for a drink tonight after work? Just to say thank you for all your help,' she added hastily.

'Hannah, that's very sweet of you, but there's really no need.'

She looked deflated and the penny dropped. Hell. The last thing he needed right now was someone with a crush on him. Not when he was still hurting so much over Miranda. 'Hannah—don't take this the wrong way, pet, but a little word of advice. Never, ever date anyone you work with. It causes too many complications later,' he said.

'Um. I... That's what Leila said.'

She'd spoken to *Leila* about him? The question must have shown in his face because she added, 'That's the Professor's official line about work and relationships.'

Yeah. He'd heard that, too. Just as well that he was no longer dating the Professor's daughter.

He pushed his own misery aside, trying not to think about Miranda and what he'd lost. Right now, Hannah needed a pep talk. She looked embarrassed and guilty and miserable. 'Hey. You're feeling awkward now and that's just talking about it. Trust me, it gets a lot worse if you actually do it. I'll forget you said anything, and we can carry right on as we are. Friends and colleagues,' he said. He added a wink. 'Plus I'm virtually a geriatric, compared to you.'

'You're only ten years older than me.'

Right now, it felt like a lifetime. He could barely remember what it was like to be twenty-two, fresh-faced and full of optimism. As if the world were your oyster. 'Old enough, pet,' he said lightly. 'Now, this ECG's an easy one to remember—it looks almost like a helix, twisting round on its axis. It's *torsade de pointes*,' he said. 'Spot that, and you need to call a specialist. Fast. And don't let them get away with trying to give you phone advice—you need someone on the spot.'

'*Torsade de pointes*,' Hannah echoed dutifully, writing it on her notepad.

Lecturing and sharing his knowledge helped. A bit. At least it kept his mind occupied. Though his body was way, way too aware of Miranda. Even with his back to the door, he knew the exact moment when she walked in. The exact moment when she left the room.

When was he ever going to lose his reaction to her?

The following day, Skip was worse. 'Let's stop the diuretics now. He needs a two-day break before we can put him on ACE inhibitors, but they should help,' he told Leila. 'In the meantime, I'll write him up for vasodilators. Keep an eye on him. If he goes into heart failure…'

Later that afternoon, Leila said to Jack, 'You've talked it up, haven't you?'

He frowned, not understanding. 'What?'

'What you said this morning about keeping an eye on Skip—about heart failure,' she reminded him. 'Skip's wheezing.'

Wheezing—sometimes called cardiac 'asthma'—was a bad sign. When Jack walked into the room, he saw that Skip's fingers were slightly blue. They also felt cool to the touch, and Skip looked ill and exhausted.

'I'm going to give you some oxygen,' he said, helping Skip to sit up. 'That'll help you breathe more easily.' Please, please, don't go into shock, he thought. If Skip went into cardiogenic shock, there was a nine out of ten chance he'd lose his patient.

He checked the monitor. The ECG was looking reasonable. Then it changed.

'He's arrested. He's in VT,' he called to Leila. 'I need you to bag him. Hannah, I need you to do chest compressions. Use the heel of your hand with straight elbow and centre it over the lower third of his sternum. Do it for a count of five then Leila will do one breath.' He counted the rhythm for her. 'Got that?'

'Got it,' Hannah said.

'Well done. Keep going.'

Skip didn't respond to the injection of adrenaline or to the CPR. 'We'll have to shock him,' Jack said. He grabbed the paddles. 'Charging to 200. And clear.' If he could correct the arrhythmia, it would buy him enough time to insert a Swan-Ganz catheter to measure the filling pressure of Skip's heart so he'd know what to give his patient to optimise the pressure—and then hopefully they'd be on their way out of the woods.

Nothing. 'And again,' he said. 'Charging to 200. And clear.'

Still nothing.

'Come on. We're not going to lose you. Come on,' he said. He had to give Skip the chance to live—to live happily without drink. 'Charging to 360. And clear.'

Still nothing.

'Keep going,' he told Leila and Hannah. 'We're going to try lignocaine.'

Still nothing.

Jack tried a different paddle position—sometimes that worked. But not today. Not for Skip.

Still nothing. Procainamide didn't work either.

'We'll try bretylium tosilate,' he said. 'Five mg per kilo of bodyweight—he's 90 kilos, so that's 450 mg. And we have to continue CPR for another twenty minutes after this. Hannah, you've done really well but you must be tired,' he continued. 'I'll give you a break.'

But twenty minutes later there was still no response. Jack knew he had to call it. His throat tightened to the point where he could barely speak. 'Time of death, three fourteen p.m.'

He walked out of the room, hardly able to see. He'd lost his patient. And it was all his fault—if he'd concentrated harder, thought more about the drugs he was prescribing, kept a closer eye on Skip's obs…

Miranda found him in her office twenty minutes later, tapping the point of his pen on a sheet of paper, making aimless dots. 'Hey. Leila's just told me.' She put a hand on his arm. 'I'm sorry.'

He shrugged it off. 'I should have bleeped you out of clinic.'

'It wouldn't have made any difference. You know his history, Jack. This was always on the cards.'

'Because he was an alcoholic?' Jack almost spat the word in disgust.

'Yes.'

Like my dad. But he couldn't say it.

'Do you want me to talk to the relatives?'

He shook his head. 'It's OK. I lost him. So I'm the one who should tell them.'

'If you want back-up support, you know where I am.'

'Yeah.'

Seeing Skip's wife and son was almost more than he could bear. 'I'm sorry,' he said. 'We did what we could. But his heart failed.'

'I told him to stop drinking. I thought if I left him, it might shock him into realising what he was doing to himself—what he was doing to *us*,' Beth Jones said. 'He just laughed, said red wine's good for the heart. I thought it'd be his liver that went, not his heart.'

Skip's son, Alistair, just looked numb. 'I can't believe he's gone. We were going sailing at the weekend. I bought this boat…' He stared at Jack. 'I never got the chance to say goodbye.'

Jack dug his nails into the palm of his hand. He knew another son of an alcoholic who'd said that. Said it sitting outside the emergency room where his father had bled to death. *I never got the chance to say goodbye.* Saying it at a funeral, at a graveside, simply wasn't the same. It wasn't the same as holding someone's hand and saying you loved them. Letting them know you'd always remember them. That they'd always be an important part of your life. *I never got the chance to say goodbye.*

When Miranda finished her shift, she walked over to Jack's house. Although it was half past nine at night, there were no lights on. Maybe he was sitting in the dark, brooding, she thought. Losing a patient didn't get any easier to deal with, no matter how long you'd been a doctor. You always mourned your patient, wondered if there was something else you could have done, some different procedure or drug you could have tried. But some cases were more personal and the loss went deeper. Skip's death had clearly hit Jack hard, and he'd looked ready to go and drown his sorrows at the end of his shift four hours before. Except Jack didn't drink. Ever.

Unless this was a first for him. Skip Jones, on top of what she'd done to him, might be enough to tip him over the edge. And for a man unused to alcohol—it didn't bear thinking about.

She shook herself. Of course Jack wouldn't do anything so reckless. And maybe this was a stupid idea. Maybe she should just leave him alone. But she couldn't stand by and just watch him suffering.

She leaned on the doorbell. No answer. Where was he? Not at Shirley's bedside—she'd checked before she'd left. With his brothers? Friends?

With a sigh she sat down on his doorstep and waited. He'd turn up eventually.

Half an hour later—when she was beginning to grow

cold—Jack walked round the corner and stopped dead. 'What are you doing here?'

'Waiting to see you. Where have you been?'

For a moment, she thought he was going to tell her it was none of her business. Then he shrugged. 'Walking. Looking at the stars.'

Brooding, he meant. 'Can I come in?'

'I don't think that's a good idea.'

Stubborn to the last. 'Jack, you've had a rough shift and you're hurting. I hate seeing you like this.'

'Yeah? So why did you dump me?'

'I can't answer that—but I had a good reason.' Miranda looked beseechingly at him. 'Trust me.'

His lip curled. 'I did. And you broke my heart.' He closed his eyes. 'I don't want to talk about it.'

'Jack, you need to talk to someone and it may as well be me. I told you about May when I lost Imogen Parker, and it helped—it helped a lot. Now let me do the same for you.'

The silence stretched on and on and on, and then at last he opened his eyes and pulled his keys from his pocket. 'All right. One coffee, and then you leave.'

She followed him inside. 'I'll make the coffee. Have you eaten tonight?'

'No, and I'm not hungry.'

'OK.' His flat tone warned her not to push too hard. She switched the kettle on and shook coffee grounds into his cafetière. 'If you won't let me feed you, you can start talking.'

'This isn't going to work.'

'It's better out than in. You know that. Come on, Jack, it's what we tell students when they lose their first patient. And it's doubly important when it's personal.'

Jack sighed. 'Yeah. You're right. Telling his family…it was just like when the consultant told us Dad was dead. Outside Resus. They'd done their best but they were sorry, they just couldn't help him in the end.'

He sat down at the kitchen table and gazed into the distance. She guessed that he was reliving the scene over and over again. She wanted to hold him close, stroke his hair and comfort him, but she knew he'd push her away. The only thing she could do for him right now was listen.

'I never got the chance to tell him how I felt. That I missed the dad I'd had as a really little kid, the one who lifted me onto his shoulders and built snowmen with me. The dad who'd read me stories. The dad who'd played cars with me, taught me to play football and let me off having my hair washed in the bath. Skip junior today… He was just the same as me. He'll always remember his dad as a sad old man who drank himself to death.'

'Hey.' She put a mug on the table in front of him. 'You remember your dad before he started drinking. Those memories are still there. Nothing's going to change the fact that you had good times, as well as bad.'

'Maybe.'

'Jack, you have to let it go.' She knew she was being hypocritical, given the Rupert situation, but she continued. 'The past is the past. Let it go.'

'Like us? It's the past, so let it go?'

She closed her eyes. 'That isn't fair.'

'On past performance, you should have had a few dates by now. Two dates per man, let's see… Oh, that must be half a dozen now at least.'

She banged her mug down hard on the table. 'Stop being so bloody—' The word 'childish' died on her lips as she realised what she'd done. 'Oh, hell. I'm sorry. I'll get a cloth and clear it up.' Coffee from the broken china seeped over the table.

'Leave it. It doesn't matter.'

'Yes, it does.' She mopped up the mess, then wiped the table clean. 'Have you got some newspaper I can wrap this in?' she asked, pointing to the broken shards.

Jack rummaged in a cupboard and found an old newspaper. He handed it to Miranda and their fingers touched. She looked up at him, her mouth parting, and suddenly the broken mug was forgotten. She was in his arms and they were kissing, touching each other, clinging on to each other for comfort, in need and desire.

She'd missed him. Missed his scent, missed the feel of his skin, missed the taste of his mouth. When he lifted her onto the kitchen worktop, she made no protest. She was too busy undoing the buttons on his shirt. When he eased her skirt up, she didn't push him away. She was too busy touching him, feeling the texture of his skin. And when he entered her, she cried out in relief and longing and need, wrapping her legs round his waist to pull him deeper.

'I've missed you,' he murmured. 'I hate going to sleep without you in my arms. I hate waking up without you. I hate having to work with you and be polite when all I really want to do is carry you off to my bed and make love to you until nothing else matters any more.' He nuzzled her cheek. 'Your skin's so soft. And I'd almost forgotten about that mole.' He touched the tip of his tongue to the tiny mole on the curve of her neck. 'And the way you feel… Oh, honey.' His voice was raw with need.

In answer, she cupped his face in her hands and kissed him.

Afterwards, Jack stared at her. 'I don't believe we just did that.'

'No.' She stroked his face. 'It wasn't supposed to get

this complicated. It was supposed to be me being professional. Helping you get over a tough time on the ward.'

'And instead we can't keep our hands off each other.' He leaned his forehead against hers. 'Guess what? It gets worse. We didn't use any protection.'

'Er—no.' She hadn't thought about that either. She'd just wanted…Jack. 'I, um, don't sleep around. So…'

'Hey.' He kissed the tip of her nose. 'I know you don't. And neither do I. I wasn't thinking about anything nasty. Just…' He paused. 'Look, I'll stand by you if there are any consequences.'

Consequences? He meant a baby. *Jack's* baby. Funny, until now she had never really given a second thought to babies. She'd always thought she was an all-out career woman. But now he'd said it… Her stomach clenched with sudden longing. What would it be like, to have Jack's baby, to feel her belly grow round with a little life? To have him rubbing the small of her back, fussing over whether her ankles were swollen or not, sitting with his hand on the bump and waiting for the baby to kick…

No. There was no point in fantasising. It wasn't going to happen. 'There won't be any consequences,' she said quietly.

He stared at her. 'Are you saying you'd have a …?' He tailed off, clearly not wanting to voice the word 'termination'.

She shook her head. 'You're a doctor. You know there's only a small window each month when a woman can get pregnant. The chances drop with age. If I were ten years younger, you could maybe start panicking. But…' No. She couldn't be feeling disappointed at the fact she probably wasn't pregnant. She couldn't *possibly*. 'If you're that worried, I could always take the morning-after pill tomorrow. Not that I'd ever recommend it to a patient as a regular form of contraception.'

'Of course.' He restored order to their clothes, then lifted her gently down from the worktop. 'So, what now?'

'I don't know, Jack.' Tears glistened in her eyes. 'Heaven help me, I still…'

'Still what?' he asked softly.

She swallowed. She couldn't say it. Couldn't say she loved him.

'You feel the same as I do, Miranda.' He curled his fingers round hers. 'We can fight it. Or maybe it would be easier to give in.'

Much, much easier to give in, she thought.

'But if we give in,' he said quietly, 'we go public.' And to hell with the Professor's unofficial edict about work and relationships. 'It's that or nothing.'

'I can't.'

'What are you hiding, Miranda?'

Demons. Ones she didn't want released. 'I can't,' she repeated.

He released her hand. 'Then I want you to leave. Now. I don't want a hole-in-the-corner relationship any more. I don't want to be anybody's grubby little secret.'

'It isn't like that.'

'Isn't it?' He turned away from her. 'Just go, Miranda.'

She wanted to hold him. To tell him she loved him. But, for his own sake, she couldn't. She couldn't risk her father ruining everything Jack had worked so hard for. Slowly, defeatedly she left and clicked the front door quietly behind her.

CHAPTER TWELVE

'JACK, phone for you,' Claire called over from the nurses' station.

'Thanks,' he called back, and picked up the extension. 'Hello, Cardiac Ward, Jack Sawyer speaking.'

'It's Ralph Turner.'

Why on earth was the Professor ringing him?

'I need to have a word with you.'

Jack's heart skipped a beat. The Professor's tone was grim, spelling trouble—but he had no idea what he'd done. 'Do you want me to come down?'

'No. I'll come up to you. Half past ten.' The professor rang off without any social chat or even a goodbye.

Hell. What had he done? Adrenaline made the back of Jack's neck feel hot. Was it to do with the party—the rumours that had doubtless gone fizzing round the marquee? Even though Les Jackson knew the truth now, mud stuck. If the Professor thought Jack had an unsavoury background and believed he wasn't morally capable of being a doctor…

No. Of course not. He was being ridiculous. Paranoid. Of course the Professor wasn't going to sack him because of a stupid rumour that had no substance to it whatsoever.

Or maybe a patient had complained. Or a family. He couldn't think of anything he'd done wrong but, if he was honest with himself, he knew he hadn't been concentrating properly on his job. Not since Miranda had walked out on him for the second time. True, he'd told her to go—but she could have said no. And putting on a polite face for the sake of the ward had put the kind of strain on him that left him unable to sleep at night.

Or maybe he was just so tired and so miserable that he was making a mountain out of a molehill.

Miranda came back from clinic and automatically looked over to the nurses' station. Jack wasn't there and she felt the familiar lurch of disappointment. It had been her choice, she reminded herself. She had to live with it. Even though she regretted it every second of the day.

She was about to go into her office when she heard a voice she recognised coming from the sister's office. She frowned. What was her father doing on the ward?

And then she realised what he was saying. She froze.

'I want you to leave Miranda alone.'

No. *No!* She'd heard those words before. Ten years before, when she'd been happy and carefree and seriously in love. This couldn't be happening. Not again. She'd given Jack up precisely so this wouldn't happen. No.

'I know you're looking for a consultant's post,' Ralph continued. 'Obviously I can't give you one here—but I can get you one elsewhere. Starting tomorrow.'

She felt sick—she really, really didn't want to hear any more—but she simply couldn't move. Her feet were too weighed down by her memories.

'Thank you.'

Oh, God. It was Rupert all over again. Give the man what he wants and he'll go away.

And then she realised that the tone was different. Not grateful, fawning. This voice was dripping with sarcasm. It wasn't thanking the professor at all. 'Yes, I do want to be a consultant. But I'll get promotion on my own merit—not because someone's put in a good word for me.'

'Of course, with two mortgages to pay, your salary has to stretch a little.'

Two mortgages? Why did Jack have two mortgages? Was he—her stomach gave another lurch—paying Jessica's mortgage? Had he been married before?

'I could do something about that. Make life a little…easier for you.'

'There's no need. I pay my own way,' Jack said. 'My salary's enough.'

'Everyone could do with a little more.'

Jack laughed mirthlessly. 'Not in my book.'

'All right. So you don't want money and you don't want promotion. What do you want?'

'Love,' Jack said.

The professor gave a short bark of laughter. 'Ridiculous.'

'No. I couldn't care less about money or social position. I don't need a flash car or a huge mansion. They're not important, compared to love. Compared to Miranda.'

Jack was standing up to her father? He wasn't just agreeing meekly and walking away with a fat cheque?

'I could make life difficult for you. Very difficult,' the professor warned.

'I'm sure you could.'

No macho posturing either.

'But my patients won't suffer for it, and neither will Miranda. Do whatever makes you happy, Professor—but don't hurt her. She deserves better.'

He was defying her father—on her behalf?

The strength suddenly returned to her legs, and she walked straight into the office without knocking.

'Do you mind? This is a private—' the professor began.

'Actually,' Miranda said, shutting the door, 'I think

this concerns me, too.' She took Jack's hand. 'As you're having a go at the man I'm going to marry.'

'You're *what*?'

'Getting married,' she said. 'Only this time you can't buy him off.'

The Professor stared at both of them. His lip curled, as if he was about to say something—and then he seemed to change his mind and simply left the room, slamming the door behind him.

'I think,' Jack said, 'we need to talk. Sooner rather than later. And not in the middle of the ward.'

She nodded. 'I'm due a break.'

'Mine's in half an hour. We're quiet this morning—'

'Don't tempt fate,' she broke in. What he'd just said virtually guaranteed an arrest before lunchtime.

He ignored her. 'I'll take my break now. Let's go for a walk.'

Once they'd sorted out their bleepers, they went out into the hospital grounds and chose a quiet spot under the may trees.

'Since when,' Jack asked, 'are we getting married?'

'Um.'

'You left me because you didn't want to go public—and now you've told your father you're going to marry me. What's going on?'

She sighed. 'It's not a pretty story.'

'I don't care. I want the truth, Miranda. All of it.'

She was silent for a long, long time. She'd never talked to anyone about what had happened with Rupert. Not even May.

'Miranda?' he prompted.

'I was engaged, about ten years ago. Rupert was a couple of years older than I was. He was a medic, too. He was the original golden boy—floppy blond hair, blue eyes, from the right sort of family.' Her lip curled. How wrong she'd been. 'We fell in love and he asked me to marry him. I thought my parents would be pleased. I knew my father wasn't happy that Rupert's father was a Lloyd's Name and had lost a fair bit of money, but I loved Rupert and I thought it wouldn't matter. And then one day Rupert was supposed to be meeting me in my room. I was late home from lectures. And I heard…' She choked. 'I heard my father paying him off. Rupert said if he gave him twenty thousand pounds, he'd break the engagement. My father gave him the cheque right there and then.'

Jack stared at her in disbelief. 'No.'

'Yes.'

'So since then you haven't trusted anyone,' Jack said. 'And that's why you won't commit to anyone, in case your father bought your lover off again.' He took her hand. 'That's why you left me?'

'I told you I wasn't good at relationships.'

'Hey. It's not your fault you picked a louse.' He traced a patter on the palm of her hand with his fingertip. 'Did you really think your father would buy me off, too?'

No, but she hadn't wanted to risk it. 'I heard what my father said to you. And it was just like Rupert.'

'I didn't sell you out,' he pointed out softly. 'And twenty thousand pounds wouldn't be anywhere near enough. You're worth… No. I can't put a price on you. Money's not important, Miranda.'

She swallowed. 'He said you were paying two mortgages.' She had to know the truth. 'Is the other one Jessica's?'

'No. It's my mum's. I suppose I wanted to give her the security she hadn't had from Dad. To pay her back for supporting me through med school. The minute I

qualified I spoke to the council about her right to buy
and arranged the mortgage.' He smiled. 'She had a bit of
a tantrum about being independent. So I got Charlie and
Brian on my side and we struck a deal. She pays what
would have been her rent into a building society account
in the name of the grandchildren, and I pay the mortgage.'

She should have guessed that Jack would do something
so unselfish. His family meant a lot to him. Whereas
hers...

'Who's Jessica, then?'

He sighed. 'I'm not good at relationships either. I met
her at university—she was doing combined arts. Marking
time, really, until she was ready to get married. She only
did enough work to stop herself getting chucked out, and
didn't take it seriously at all. I fell in love with her—she
looked like an angel. And even though she was from a
posh family and I was nowhere near her social class, I
thought she'd fallen in love with me.'

And he thought he'd made the same mistake with
Miranda. Fallen in love with someone way out of his
social class.

'I wanted to marry her. I knew we'd have to wait until
I'd qualified, but I wanted the world to know she was
mine. I even bought her an engagement ring. It wasn't
an expensive one, but it was all I could afford. I thought
the fact I loved her would be enough. I could buy her
something more expensive later when I'd qualified and
had moved a few rungs up the career ladder. I was on
my way to propose when I heard her talking to some
friends.' He dropped Miranda's hand. 'She said I was fun
for now, but not the kind of man you'd marry.'

'She said *what*?' Miranda asked, outraged.

'I didn't take it very well either.' He smiled ruefully.

'I hadn't even given her the ring. I could have taken it back to the shop and got my money back—but I didn't want anyone knowing what a fool I'd been. I went down to the river and threw the ring as far as I could into the water. And I decided then I wouldn't have another serious relationship until I'd made consultant.'

'And then we met.'

'And my good intentions went straight out of the window.'

'So did mine.' She sighed. 'I just wanted to protect you from my father.'

'Maybe,' Jack said softly, 'he realised Rupert wasn't what you thought he was and was trying to protect you.'

'No. My father's a control freak. He just had these set ideas about what I should and shouldn't do.'

'So where do we go from here?' Jack asked.

Miranda looked at him. 'You told my father you loved me.'

'Yes.'

'And…' Say it. It's safe now, she reminded herself. Say it. 'I love you.'

Jack said nothing.

Panic began to gallop through her veins. No. It couldn't be too late. 'Will…' It felt as if she were speaking through a mouthful of treacle. 'Will you marry me?'

'No.'

Her eyes widened in shock. 'But…'

'No. You're not asking me for the right reasons,' Jack said. 'And until you've sorted things out with your father, you're always going to be panicking about what he'll do next. You won't be able to trust anyone. You won't be able to let yourself *really* love.'

'So you don't want to marry me.'

'That's not what I said. You need to talk to your father. Give him a chance to explain why he did it.'

'He doesn't do explanations.'

'Then he'll have to learn,' Jack said implacably. 'Because without understanding, this relationship's going nowhere.'

'Ally, is my father free?' Miranda asked.

'He's working on a report. And he's not in the best of moods,' Ally warned.

'Please?'

'On your head be it,' the secretary said with a rueful smile.

Miranda rapped on the door.

'Yes,' Ralph barked.

She walked in and closed the door behind her. 'I know you're busy, but I just need five minutes.'

His eyes narrowed. 'If you've come to—'

'Have a row?' she cut in. 'No, Dad. I haven't.'

He stared at her. 'You haven't called me "Dad" in years.'

'No.' Not since he'd bought off her fiancé. 'Um—can I sit down?'

'Is this about Jack Sawyer?'

'Yes and no.' She sighed. 'I need to know—why did you do it? Rupert, I mean.'

'He wasn't right for you.'

'Because his family lost all their money?'

Ralph shook his head. 'Rupert was weak and greedy, just like his father. And I didn't want you to have that sort of life. I didn't want you married to someone who'd only make you miserable.'

'You could have told me.'

Ralph smiled wryly. 'Miranda, you wouldn't have listened. You were so headstrong you would probably have rushed out and married him on the spot.' He sighed. 'You were so confident, but so young and naïve… Maybe your mother and I sheltered you too much.'

'You wanted a son, not a daughter.'

'Yes, I wanted a son,' he admitted, and her heart squeezed painfully. She'd thought for years he hadn't wanted her. And now she knew. He'd told her straight. He really, really hadn't wanted her.

'Did you hear what I just said?' he demanded.

'Hear what?' she asked dully.

'I didn't think you were listening. I said, I wanted a son *as well as* my daughter.'

So he *had* wanted her?'

'It wasn't to be. Milly had three miscarriages and we agreed we couldn't face any more. But, believe me, we always wanted you. Always.'

'You didn't want me to be a doctor.'

'I didn't want you to go into a job where you had no sleep, worked ridiculous hours and got treated like dirt by senior consultants who still lived in the Dark Ages. Consultants like me,' he said. 'I wanted you to have a job where people would make a fuss of you. Where you'd be cherished as much as we cherished you. But you were set on it, and then May egged you on.'

'May supported me,' she said.

'Not all on her own. Your, um, mother helped out a bit.'

'What? But she wanted me to—'

'Be like her? Yes, but she realised in the end that wasn't what you wanted. And May said if we let you go, maybe one day you'd come back to us.'

'You hardly ever rang me.'

'You wanted to be independent. But May told us how you were getting on.'

'You didn't even come to my graduation.'

'We didn't think you wanted us there,' he said softly.

'I did.' Miranda choked back the threatening tears. 'And you didn't want me to have the job here, even though I'd worked hard enough, was good enough at my job to be a consultant.'

'I know you are. Your work at Glasgow was excellent. Which was why I recommended you to the board—even though I didn't officially have any power to vote.'

She stared at him. 'But…'

'How could I tell you?' he asked softly. 'Every time I came near you, you bit my head off.'

True enough, she acknowledged. 'So why did you try to buy Jack off?'

'Because you've looked so unhappy lately—and I heard on the grapevine that you'd been seeing each other.'

'I broke it off with him. I thought you'd try to come between us. Because he's not from the right background—because of what Les Jackson said about his mother.' And she didn't say it but they both knew it. *Because of what he'd done with Rupert.*

Ralph smiled thinly. 'Do you really think I'm that much of a snob? And when you can actually make out what Les Jackson says—' to Miranda's shock, Ralph lapsed into a passable imitation of Les's upper-class mumbling '—it's usually a load of rubbish.'

'We've really misunderstood each other,' she said.

'Yes.'

'I'm sorry.'

'So am I. I lost my little girl ten years ago.' He

shrugged. 'And your mother's no better. She doesn't know how to reach you either.'

'If I'd thought you loved me. That you wanted me to be happy…'

'We do, Miranda. We just didn't want to see you get hurt. I suppose we wanted to protect you from the world.'

'I needed to learn from my own mistakes.'

'I realise that now,' Ralph said.

'So—can we start again?'

He held out his arms and, for the first time in over a decade, Miranda hugged her father.

'I don't agree with mixing work and relationships,' he said, 'because I've seen too many good working relationships turn sour after the romance fades out, and too many patients suffering the consequences. But if you want to marry Jack Sawyer,' he added softly, 'you have my blessing. He's a good man. But promise me you'll only marry him if you're really sure.'

Oh, I'm sure, Miranda thought. But that wasn't the real 'if'. 'If he'll have me,' she whispered.

Pick me up at 7 tonight. Miranda pressed the 'send' key and waited.

Ten minutes later, her computer beeped. *Where are we going?*

Exclusive restaurant, she sent back.

Jack's reply was simply an exclamation mark.

And at precisely seven o'clock that evening her doorbell rang. Miranda rushed to open the door. Jack stood there, holding a bouquet of exquisite white lilies.

'Thank you,' she said. She ushered him in and put the lilies into a vase.

'Did you talk to your father?'

She nodded. 'I learned a lot. Let's just say there have

been a few misunderstandings over the years. If we'd talked, we'd have sorted it out.'

'So much for you being the queen of straight talking,' he said. 'And now?'

'We're building bridges. It'll take time, but we're going to try.' She paused. 'He likes you, you know.'

Jack raised an eyebrow. 'It didn't feel that way earlier today. Or was that some obscure kind of test?'

'He'd heard on the grapevine that we'd been seeing each other. He thought you were making me unhappy.'

'Funny, that. I thought it was the other way round.' Jack ran his fingers through her hair. 'You ought to tie this back.'

'Why?'

'It's too distracting.'

She grinned. 'If I put it back, you'd spend all evening wanting to let it down again.'

'True.' Jack continued playing with her hair. 'So. What now?'

'Elizabeth Barrett Browning,' she said.

'That's my line. You'll have to be more original than that.'

'Will you marry me?'

'Nope. That's my line, too.'

Miranda went very still. 'Is it?'

He leaned forward and kissed the tip of her nose. 'But there are some ground rules. Number one, no engagement ring.'

'What's this, then?' She took her hand and guided it under her shirt to her midriff.

'A non-engagement ring.' He removed his hand. 'Stop distracting me. I need to be able to think straight. No engagement ring—that was Rupert and Jessica and they're both in the past. And they're staying there.'

'Agreed.'

He smiled. 'I'll buy you an eternity ring on our first wedding anniversary.'

'So we're going to get married, then?'

'I haven't finished the ground rules yet. Number two. Sonia makes the wedding rings.'

'Sonia?'

He slid his fingers under her shirt and circled her navel. 'She of the purple gold.'

'OK.'

'Number three. We keep the grannies busy.'

'Grannies?'

'Our mothers.'

The penny dropped. 'Babies?'

'Mmm-hmm. We just cross our fingers that our daughters don't inherit your stubbornness gene.'

'Or our sons inherit yours,' she retorted crisply.

He grinned. 'And if they do...I think one of each might be more than enough to keep the grannies busy.'

'Babies. And you're expecting me to give up work?'

'No. You do what makes you happy—full time, part time, whatever. The same goes for me. We'll work out a compromise, as a *family*,' he reminded her. 'Number four. You improve your poetry collection.'

'I might need a bit of help with that. Personal tuition,' she emphasised.

'Done.'

'Any more rules?'

'Just one more question.' He dropped to one knee and brought her left hand to his lips. 'Miranda—will you marry me?'

Slowly, she drew him to his feet. Slid her arms round his neck. Kissed him lingeringly...and whispered the word they both wanted to hear. 'Yes.'

Watch out for exciting new covers on your favourite books!

Every month we bring you romantic fiction that you love!
Now it will be even easier to find your favourite book with our **fabulous new covers!**

We've listened to you – our loyal readers, and as of **July publications** you'll find that...

We've improved:

☑ *Variety between the books*
☑ *Ease of selection*
☑ *Flashes or symbols to highlight mini-series and themes*

We've kept:

☑ *The familiar cover colours*
☑ *The series names you know*
☑ *The style and quality of the stories you love*

Be sure to look out for next months titles so that you can preview our exciting new look.

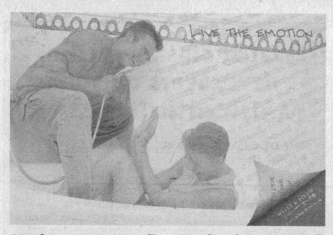

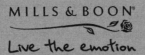

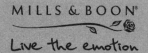

4 FREE

books and a surprise gift!

We would like to take this opportunity to thank you for reading this Mills & Boon® book by offering you the chance to take FOUR more specially selected titles from the Medical Romance™ series absolutely FREE! We're also making this offer to introduce you to the benefits of the Reader Service™—

- ★ FREE home delivery
- ★ FREE gifts and competitions
- ★ FREE monthly Newsletter
- ★ Exclusive Reader Service offers
- ★ Books available before they're in the shops

Accepting these FREE books and gift places you under no obligation to buy, you may cancel at any time, even after receiving your free shipment. Simply complete your details below and return the entire page to the address below. *You don't even need a stamp!*

YES! Please send me 4 free Medical Romance books and a surprise gift. I understand that unless you hear from me, I will receive 6 superb new titles every month for just £2.69 each, postage and packing free. I am under no obligation to purchase any books and may cancel my subscription at any time. The free books and gift will be mine to keep in any case.

M4ZED

Ms/Mrs/Miss/Mr ....Initials................................
BLOCK CAPITALS PLEASE

Surname ....

Address ....

....

....Postcode................................

Send this whole page to:
UK: FREEPOST CN81, Croydon, CR9 3WZ
EIRE: PO Box 4546, Kilcock, County Kildare (stamp required)